DAN FREEDMAN

SCHOLASTIC

First published in the UK in 2008 by Scholastic Children's Books
An imprint of Scholastic Ltd
Euston House, 24 Eversholt Street
London, NW1 1DB, UK
Registered office: Westfield Road, Southam, Warwickshire, CV47 0RA

ISBN 978 1407 10294 8

A CIP catalogue record for this book is available from the British Library

Printed in the UK by CPI Bookmarque, Croydon, Surrey
Papers used by Scholastic Children's Books are made from wood grown in sustainable forests.

1 3 5 7 9 10 8 6 4 2

www.scholastic.co.uk/zone

Acknowledgements

Thanks to:

Mum and Ivan for your honesty.

Dad for taking me to football.

Sir Trevor Brooking for your time and your vision.

Hazel Ruscoe; this is inspired by the ideas we had together.

Ena McNamara and Oli Karger for your invaluable advice.

Gary Lineker for your support.

Jon & Phil for being there every step of the way and Joanne for being lovely.

Caspian Dennis and Lola Cashman for your belief in me.
Elv Moody and the fantastic team at Scholastic for everything you have done to get this book into people's hands...

Part
One
The Semi-Final

1 Semi Conscious

Thursday 22 May

INTERSCHOOL CUP SEMI-FINAL
35:00 MINS PLAYED
KINGFIELD 0 OAK HALL 0

Jamie flung his body across the turf to make the tackle. He had tracked the Oak Hall midfielder all the way and, when the time was right, he'd made his move.

But Jamie Johnson was not a defender and he never would be.

Jamie was the best left-winger in the whole of Kingfield school. He had the pace to beat any defender.

So why was Mr Hansard playing him at wing back? And how could he do it in a game as important as the Interschool Cup Semi-Final?

It was stupid. Pointless.

Jamie should have been Kingfield's most dangerous weapon, not the one doing all the defending. If they were going to go out of the Cup, they should at least go out trying to win the game.

It was 0 – 0 and, with ten minutes left until half-time, Jamie realized that the Oak Hall keeper hadn't made one save yet. It was actually embarrassing.

Jamie looked at the crowd watching the game from the touchline. There were probably about a hundred people there. He dreaded to think what they were making of Kingfield's long-ball tactics.

There had been a few whispers that some scouts from professional clubs might be coming to check Jamie out today. But even if any of them *had* turned up, there was no way they could have been impressed by a winger who wasn't allowed to enter the opposition half.

It was as if Mr Hansard wanted to play him so deep that no one would spot his talent.

Jamie wiped his shirtsleeve across his forehead to soak up the sweat. He was waiting impatiently for Oak Hall to take their throw-in.

Deep down, he knew this cup run might be his last

chance of earning a trial with a professional club. He was fourteen. If it didn't happen now, it probably never would. It was time for him to show what he could do.

2

On the Run

Jamie anticipated what was going to happen. He raced to intercept the Oak Hall throw-in and won possession of the ball.

If he was going to stick to Hansard's tactics, Jamie now had to whack the ball into the channel for Ashish Khan to chase. But Jamie didn't feel like sticking to the plan.

Jamie pushed the ball a good ten yards in front of him so he could really open up his stride. As soon as he started running, his pace kicked in; he rocketed down the line. The Oak Hall right back came across to close him down but Jamie just flew past him.

He felt his marker try to clip his ankle and it would have been a free-kick . . . if Jamie had gone down. But he didn't. He wasn't going to stop now; he just kept on running.

Jamie drove further and further forward, deep into the heart of Oak Hall territory. As he approached the penalty area, the crowd on the touchline strained their necks to keep up with the action. Now they were seeing the *real* Jamie Johnson.

One more defender – that's all Jamie had to beat.

"Yes! Play me!" shouted Ash. He was the only player who'd been quick enough to keep up with Jamie. He was making a run across the box to the penalty spot.

Jamie looked up and shaped to cross it to Ash; that's exactly what everyone would be expecting him to do. But Jamie wanted to do something a little bit more special than that. He wanted to do something for any of the scouts that might be there. He wanted to go all the way himself.

Jamie put his head down and dashed towards the last Oak Hall defender. When he got close enough, he moved his left foot over the ball with a flourish to make it seem as though he was going to go on the outside. Then, just as the defender closed him down, he pushed the ball inside with his right foot to head straight for goal.

It was a classic step-over. There was just one problem: the defender didn't buy it. He'd stayed on his feet and kept his eye on the ball. He tackled Jamie just as he was on the brink of a brilliant individual goal.

Jamie squeezed his eyes shut and threw his head up to

the sky. "Aaagh!" he growled in anguish. He'd been so close. Why didn't his step-over work? All the best wingers were wicked at step-overs. . .

"Johnson!!" Hansard roared from the sidelines. "Get baaack!!"

Jamie turned around to see that the defender that had tackled him was now leading an Oak Hall counter-attack. There was a huge gap down Kingfield's left flank – exactly where Jamie should have been.

With no one to mark him, the Oak Hall player had been able to get all the way to the edge of the penalty area, from where he delivered a sumptuous curling cross to the far post.

The ball sailed effortlessly over all the Kingfield defenders' heads, finding its target of the tall Oak Hall striker. The attacker sprang high into the air and pulled his head back before jerking it forward again with power and precision to fire the ball across the goal towards the far corner of the net.

Jamie had only got back as far as the halfway line. He was still out of breath from his own run. As his lungs panted their exhaustion, he knew that Hansard would blame him for this goal. He could already hear the abuse coming his way.

But then Calum Fogarty, the Kingfield goalkeeper, flew into the air, clawing towards the ball like an eagle swooping for its prey. He got the ends of his fingertips to it, and touched it around the post for the corner.

He hadn't just saved a goal. He'd saved Jamie too.

"Johnson!" bellowed Hansard. He sounded more like an army general than a football coach. "Get back and defend the corner! Play for the team, not for yourself!"

"You tell him, sir!" shouted Dillon Simmonds, Jamie's biggest enemy on the team. "It's like we're playing with ten men!"

Jamie sprinted back towards his goal. If they wanted to see how fast he could run, he'd show them. Why was it always him that they had a go at? Why couldn't they pick on someone else for a change?

And what did either of them know about football anyway?

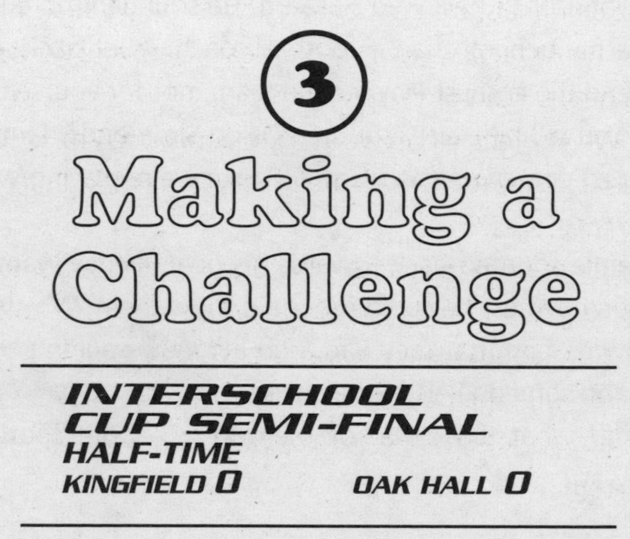

It was boiling hot as Hansard pulled his team around him for the half-time team-talk. Jamie could taste the salty sweat seeping into his mouth. He could feel the heat radiating from his forehead without even touching it.

Maybe he felt the heat more than the others because his skin was so fair.

"OK. Apart from *one or two* certain individuals who seem to think that they are *too good* to stick to the tactics, things are going to plan," said Hansard, staring right at Jamie as he spoke. He had that same look on his face – as if he'd just tasted some milk that had gone sour – that he got whenever he looked at Jamie.

"Semi-finals are about seeing who cracks first. If we stick to my tactics, we'll keep a clean sheet and we'll win this game. I can promise you that.

"We protect what we've got and hit them on the counter. They're mentally frail. They will break. I can see it in their eyes."

With the sun reflecting off the top of Hansard's head, it looked like a newly polished cue ball on a pool table.

"Is everybody clear on the tactics?" he said.

"Yes, sir," the boys answered robotically.

"Good. Has anyone got anything they want to say?" he asked, looking at Dillon, who was the captain.

"Sir, I have. . ."

As his teammates looked round at him in surprise, Jamie realized that he was the one who was talking. His friend Ollie Walsh was shaking his head at Jamie, trying to tell him not to carry on. But Jamie had already started.

"If we can get it to my feet . . . I can get past their defenders easily," he said. "Can we play it on the ground a bit more?"

Hansard stared at Jamie as if he'd suggested that they all get different outfits and play the second half in fancy dress.

"I'm sorry, Johnson – for a second I thought I was the coach of this football team!" Hansard snarled. "You've already nearly cost us a goal through your selfishness and now you're trying to tell me how to do my job. . ."

"But, sir!" Jamie said, feeling Ollie's elbow dig into his ribs. They knew Hansard hated being interrupted. Still, it was too late now.

"All these long balls . . . we just keep giving it away. How can we score a goal if we haven't got the ball?"

"Fine," said Hansard in a much calmer voice than Jamie had expected. "No problem at all . . . if you don't like my tactics, Johnson, you don't have to use them. Walker, get warmed up, you're coming on."

4
Watching On

Jamie's mouth hung open. Hansard couldn't just take him off! Not Jamie. And not in a match this big.

He was committing football suicide!

"Sir, I was just giving my opinion, I thought. . ."

"And what's so special about your opinion, Johnson? Do you think you're better than everyone else?"

"No, sir, I just. . ."

"How do you spell team, Johnson?"

"Erm . . . T, E, A, M, sir."

"Exactly. There is no *I* in team, Johnson – and you can think about that during the second half," he said, turning his back on Jamie.

"Exactly," Dillon Simmonds parroted, smiling sarcastically at Jamie.

"Now," said Hansard. "Has anybody else got any comments to make about my tactics?"

As the ref blew his whistle to get the second half under way, Jamie was torn in hundreds of different directions. Part of him wanted Kingfield to lose really badly so everyone could see what a fool Hansard had been to sub him. But, then again, Jamie knew that the only way he was going to play in the Cup Final was if Kingfield went on to win without him.

He couldn't bear the thought of just being an onlooker when he should have been out there playing. He thought about walking off to go and see how Jack was doing. She was in goal for Kingfield's girls' team, who were playing their own Cup Semi-Final at the other end of the fields.

At least he would be appreciated there; she would love it if he went over to support her.

But then Jamie thought about how bad it looked when professional players who had been substituted just disappeared down the tunnel instead of staying to support their team. It seemed as if they didn't care about the game, only about themselves.

Jamie didn't want people to think that about him. He *did* care. He cared more than anyone.

In the end, Jamie poked his foot into the black plastic bag by the side of the pitch and dragged out one of the footballs they had used for the warm-up. He rolled the ball between his feet as made his way around the pitch to where his granddad, Mike, was standing.

As far back as Jamie could remember, Mike had watched every single game that Jamie had ever played. He loved talking about football and always got into conversations with some of the other boys' dads. Today, though, Jamie didn't recognize the two smartly dressed men that Mike was talking to.

When he saw Jamie coming, Mike said goodbye to the other men and walked towards his grandson.

"How come you're off, JJ? Did you pick up a knock?" Mike asked. Jamie could tell he was worried. His forehead was rumpled across the middle. That only happened when he was concerned.

"Nope," said Jamie. He kept his eyes fixed on the ball as he rolled it back and forth under the sole of his boot; he was embarrassed. Mike had been such a good player that he had probably never been subbed in his whole career. It made Jamie being hauled off at half-time seem even worse.

"What? So he hooked you, did he?"

Jamie nodded.

He and Mike turned to see what was happening in the match. They let their disappointed silence fill the air as they watched Dillon Simmonds jump highest to make a headed clearance.

The ball skipped out of play and sped straight at Mike. But he didn't move. Or even alter his stance. He just let the ball bounce up on to his thigh before softly volleying it with his instep perfectly into the path of the Oak Hall winger who had come across to take the throw.

The Oak Hall player looked at Mike for a second to make sure that what he thought he'd seen had actually happened. Had this old man just produced the best bit of skill anyone had seen the whole afternoon?

Of course he had. What the Oak Hall player didn't know was that forty years ago, this "old man" was a professional player with Hawkstone United and was rated as one of the best teenagers in the whole country. His knee injuries may have forced him to retire before he was twenty but, even now, Mike Johnson still had the touch of a professional. And everyone had just seen it.

For a second, as he looked at Mike, Jamie felt a swell of pride. But it was soon drowned by a wave of doubt rising up within him.

Now the same dark questions that always haunted him gathered once again around his mind: was it too late for him? Was his dream of following in Mike's footsteps and becoming a professional footballer only a stupid fantasy? Was he going to be a . . . failure?

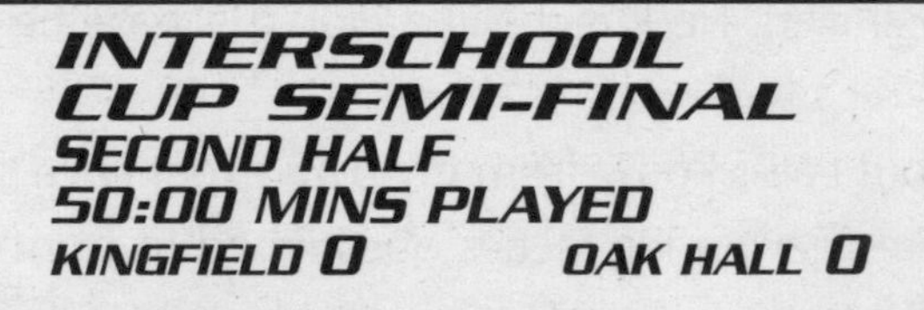

As an Oak Hall player did a neat back-heel, drawing applause from the crowd, Jamie's frustration began to accelerate into anger. He should still be out there; he should be the one that people were clapping for.

If Kingfield ended up losing this Semi-Final and Jamie missed his chance to prove himself on the big stage, he would never forgive Hansard.

"All I said was that we should try and keep the ball

instead of hoofing it the whole time!" Jamie said to Mike, half-explaining, half-apologizing for being substituted.

"Hmmm," Mike responded, taking in Jamie's words like a detective slowly putting together the clues of a crime. All the time, his eyes were flickering from side to side, tracking the action on the pitch.

"What?" Jamie snapped. "What's wrong with that? You think he's right to sub me? For that?! That's a load of. . ."

"I haven't said anything, JJ! You know I'll never agree with anyone who subs you . . ."

Jamie smiled. He knew Mike would always be on his side.

". . . but I also know from my own experience that no coach likes having his tactics questioned in front of the rest of the team. It sounds to me like he wanted to make an example of you so everyone knows who's boss."

"Yeah, but Mr Marsden never had to do *that*! And we still knew he was the boss."

Jamie wished Mr Marsden was still coaching the team. He always encouraged Jamie; and when he called Jamie his "secret weapon" and his "pocket rocket", it used to make Jamie play even better.

After one of Mr Marsden's pep talks, Jamie felt he could terrorize any defence. Even if they put two men on him, he just took it as a compliment and tried to beat both of them!

It had been a disaster when it came out that Mr Marsden and Ollie Walsh's mum had been having an affair. At first Marsden had tried to carry on as normal but when the other mums – who were probably just jealous – went to see the head teacher, Mr Patten, about it, the gossiping started to sweep through the school like a plague.

It was in his team-talk just before Kingfield's first tie in this Interschool Cup run that Mr Marsden had told the boys that he was moving schools.

"It's not that I want to," he'd said. "It's just that, with the way things are here, I don't think I can do my job properly any more. I'm sorry, guys; you're one of the best teams that I've ever worked with. I wouldn't be at all surprised if you go on and win this cup."

The last thing he'd said to them in that team-talk was: "You don't need tactics from me today – just go out there and enjoy yourselves."

When he'd finished talking, all the boys started clapping.

That day, Kingfield won their match 5 – 2. It could have been ten. Jamie scored two goals. The second was a beautiful left-footed volley from just outside the area. It was the type of strike that the TV pundits would have called a contender for Goal of the Season.

When it went in, Jamie dashed straight over to celebrate with Mr Marsden.

"That one's for you, sir," he'd said.

Mr Marsden left the school the next day. The boys were told that a Mr Hansard – who had been the Kingfield football coach before Mr Marsden joined – would be returning to take over.

The day that Mr Hansard walked back into Kingfield School was the day that everything changed for Jamie. But not for the better.

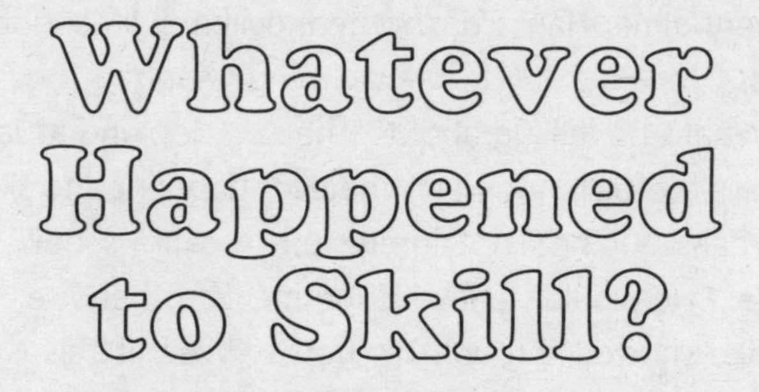

INTERSCHOOL CUP SEMI-FINAL
75:00 MINS PLAYED
KINGFIELD 0 OAK HALL 0

Jamie and Mike continued to watch the game from the sidelines. It was a tight match; still no goals and only fifteen minutes left.

Both teams seemed content to keep clearing the ball as far as they could up the pitch – happy just to make sure their goal was not under threat. Hardly anyone was taking the time to control the ball.

Hansard was prowling up and down the touchline, continuously cupping his hands around his mouth to bellow instructions at his players.

"Grind it out!" he yelled. "Win your battles!"

The vein in his temple throbbed with each shouted order.

Every time Hansard shouted, Mike just shook his head.

"What's he talking about?" he said, looking at Jamie. "This is football, not war. Whatever happened to skill?"

"Yeah, but he's not interested in skill, is he?" said Jamie. "He wouldn't have taken me off otherwise."

Mike snorted through his nose. "Well, if this is Plan A," he said, "I'd hate to see Plan B."

At that moment, Hansard turned around and stared, first at Jamie and then at Mike. It was almost as if he'd heard their entire conversation. Jamie could see the anger burning in Hansard's eyes.

At first, Jamie thought that Hansard was annoyed with him again, but then he noticed that it was Mike he seemed to be preoccupied with. Mike and Hansard were glaring at each other like two boxers trying to stare each other out before a fight.

For a couple of seconds, time seemed to stand still.

Jamie wasn't sure what was going on; all he knew was that he had never seen this look in his granddad's eye before.

Then Hansard turned away to hurl another command at his team.

"What's his problem?" Jamie whispered to Mike, who had still not taken his eyes off Hansard.

"He's forgotten how to enjoy football."

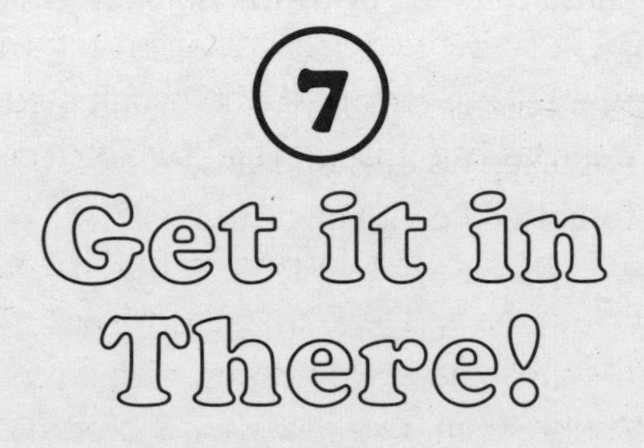

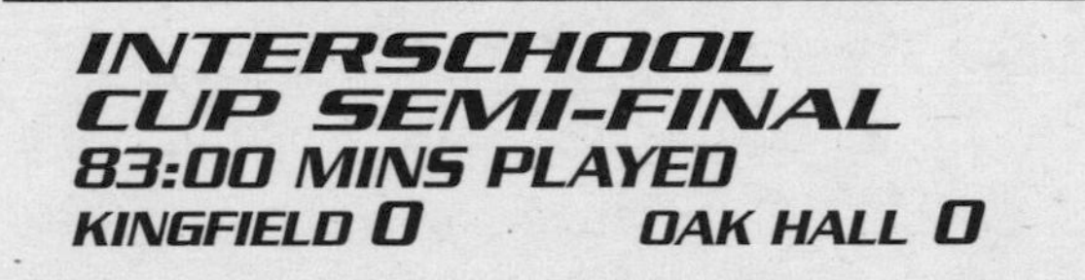

Jamie looked at Mike's watch. There were seven minutes left. He wondered which team would have more energy in extra-time.

Kingfield had won a throw-in level with the Oak Hall penalty area. Ollie Walsh sprinted over to take it.

"Get it in there!" Hansard was shouting, pointing towards the penalty area. Ollie nodded. He wiped his hands on his top to get rid of the sweat. Then he picked up the ball and took a couple of steps back before running forward and releasing it.

Ollie had the longest throw in the whole school – the ball went all the way to the edge of the area. This was one of the moves that Hansard had worked on in training and, sure enough, Dillon Simmonds, who had pushed forward into the Oak Hall half, made a late, surging run towards the ball.

"Dillon's!" he shouted, leaping to flick the ball on. It went high into the air above the penalty spot.

While the other players looked up, waiting for the ball to drop, Ashish Khan, Kingfield's top scorer this season, went to meet it. With his back to the goal, he sprang towards the sky. In mid-air, he straightened his body completely, as though he were lying on an invisible bed. Then, as the ball fell towards him, he thrashed his right foot up and over his head.

His foot – now directly above his head – made powerful contact with the ball, firing it back towards the goal behind him.

It was the perfect overhead kick. As gravity reclaimed Ash, pulling him groundwards, his shot crashed into the underside of the crossbar with so much force that the ball bounced down on to the goal-line and then right back up again into the roof of the net.

The players' brains took a second to process everything

that their eyes had shown them. Then they realized; it was in!

Ash had scored!

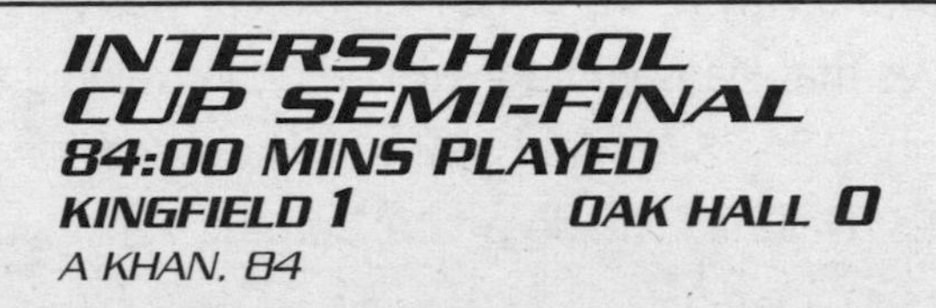
INTERSCHOOL
CUP SEMI-FINAL
84:00 MINS PLAYED

KINGFIELD 1	OAK HALL 0
A KHAN. 84	

Jamie and Mike both leapt off the ground, along with the rest of the Kingfield supporters.

Whatever Jamie thought of him, Hansard's plan had paid off.

Kingfield were on their way to the Interschool Cup Final.

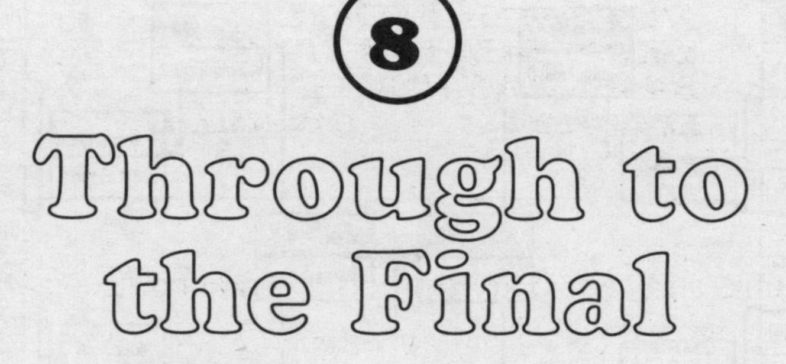

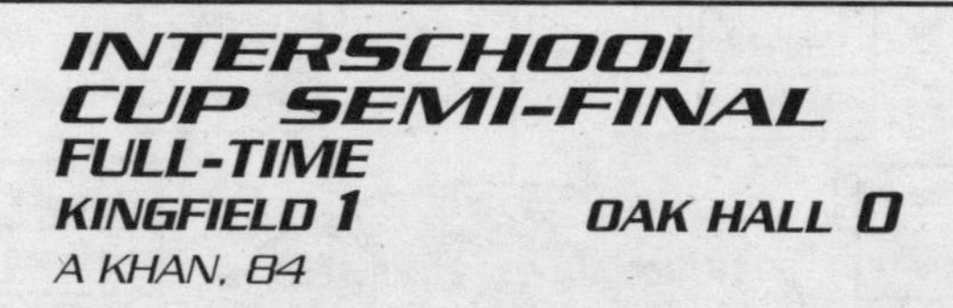

KINGFIELD SCHOOL REACH INTERSCHOOL CUP FINAL

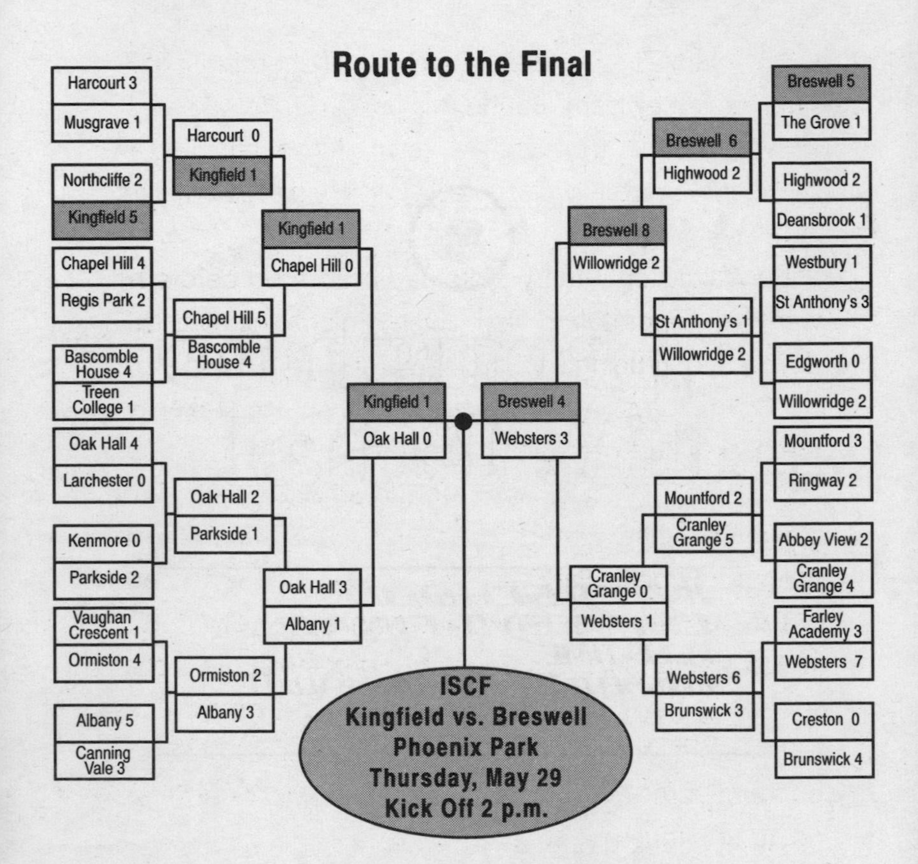

"You get on there and enjoy it," Mike said to Jamie. The full-time whistle had just blown and all the Kingfield boys were celebrating together in a huddle. "Go on!"

Jamie wandered on to the pitch, leaving Mike to talk to the two blokes that he'd been chatting with earlier.

"We're gonna win the Cup! We're gonna win the

Cup!" Jamie's teammates were half-shouting, half-singing as they leapt around in a big circle.

Even though this was his team, Jamie felt like an outsider. He certainly didn't feel as if he'd played any part in their victory.

He waited until the huddle had broken up before he went to congratulate Ash. Even though he was still devastated at being subbed, he was happy for Ash.

"Oh my days, Ash!" he said, slapping the striker on the back. "Best overhead I've ever seen!"

"Cheers, JJ," said Ash, a wide smile revealing his gleaming white teeth. "Your turn in the final – you ready for Phoenix Park?"

This year the Cup Final was going to be played at a proper stadium. The boys had been buzzing about it ever since they had looked up a picture of Phoenix Park on the Internet a couple of weeks ago. Jamie's whole body pulsated at the thought of running out there. Now it was going to happen!

"Ready?" he said. "I was born ready!"

Then Jamie jogged over to do a high five with Ollie. Their hands met with a firm connection. Ollie was easily his best mate on the team – he always made Jamie laugh.

"Great long throw, Ol," Jamie said. "It went as far as a corner!"

"Yeah? Well, it's all down to these special exercises I've got for my wrists," said Ollie, grinning. "Eh – the gaffer doesn't mind the spotlight, does he?"

Ollie was pointing to Hansard, who was having his picture taken by a photographer. He had his fists clenched and was looking straight down the lens of the camera.

Jamie realized this was the first time he'd ever seen Hansard smile. Normally he was angry, and usually with Jamie. Even the other boys had noticed it; it was as if Mr Hansard had hated Jamie from the day he'd first set eyes on him.

"OK – can I get all the Kingfield lads in for a team shot, please?" the photographer said loudly after he'd finished with Hansard. He had the kind of voice that you could hear from miles away.

"Are we gonna be in the paper?" asked Ollie.

"Course you are," said the photographer, arranging the boys into two rows. "There's going to be a big splash in the *Advertiser* tomorrow."

"Wicked!" said Ollie, clicking his fingers together. "Wait till the girls see this!"

"OK," said the photographer. "When I count to three, I want you all to say Cup Final as loud as you can! And lots of cheeky smiles! OK, here we go. . . One, two, three. . ."

"CUP FINAL!!!" The boys shouted as loud as they

could and, in their minds, every single one of them imagined lifting that trophy at Phoenix Park in seven days' time.

Then all the boys sprang off in different directions, looking for someone else to share their excitement with.

Jamie looked for Mike. He was still talking to the same two men. The men were nodding to each other now as they pointed towards Dillon and started to walk towards him.

"So your picture's going to be in the paper then, Jamie?" said Mike, patting Jamie on the back. "First of many, I reckon."

"I hope so!" said Jamie. For a second, he allowed images of stardom and celebrity to sparkle in his mind. Money, cars and parties all whizzed though his imagination. Jack had always told him he was going to be famous. Maybe she was right. Maybe the Cup Final at Phoenix Park would be where it would all start for him.

"Who are those two?" Jamie asked, pointing to the two men who were now talking to Dillon. "Are they from the *Advertiser*?"

"No," said Mike. "They're scouts."

9 Hawk Eye

Jamie couldn't believe it when Mike told him. It just seemed so unfair.

The two men that had spoken to Dillon after the game *were* football scouts. And not just any old scouts. They were from Hawkstone United – the club that Mike had played for and that Jamie had supported all his life.

"What?!" Jamie said, trying to make sense of all the scrambled thoughts suddenly scurrying around his mind. "Hawkstone scouts were here today? Mike! Why didn't you tell me?"

"I knew you'd try too hard, Jamie. The best way for you to impress is to just play your natural game."

"Yeah, but if I'd known *they* were here, I wouldn't

have started gobbing off at half-time and got myself substituted, would I?"

"It's not the end of the world, Jamie, there are plenty of other. . ."

". . .Now I'll probably never play for Hawkstone . . . and *he* will."

After the game, Dillon positioned himself outside the dressing rooms to make sure that everyone could hear as he broadcast his news.

"They said I'm strong and brave," he boasted. "Right in the Hawkstone mould. . . Think about it – all you lot can say that you played in the same school team as Dillon Simmonds when you're older."

The other boys were crowding around him, asking questions. "When's the trial?", "How much money are you going to get?" They had already all started to suck up to him.

Jamie pushed his way past the scrum around Dillon. As far as he was concerned, this couldn't have happened to a worse person. He and Dillon had always been enemies since Dillon had started picking on Jamie on his very first day at Kingfield. And things had got even worse recently, with Dillon trying it on with Jack the whole time. Jamie knew Dillon was just doing it to make him jealous but that didn't make it any easier to take.

And now Hawkstone – the team that Jamie had always felt he was destined to play for – had asked Dillon to go for a trial! Jamie couldn't bear it. And what made it all more infuriating than anything else was the fact that, deep down, Jamie knew he was a better player than Dillon.

Dillon was a bully – Jamie was a footballer.

If Hawkstone were going to sign a player from Kingfield School it should have been Jamie. Not Dillon. Anyone but Dillon.

As he waited to meet Jack so they could walk home together, Jamie realized something horrible: today could so easily have been the best day of his life. If things had gone differently, he could have stayed on and played brilliantly in the second half, inspiring Kingfield to the Cup Final and earning himself a trial with Hawkstone United in the process.

Instead, he'd been substituted in the biggest match of his life and the person he hated most in the world had stolen his chance of becoming a professional footballer.

How had it all gone so wrong?

And why?

10 Jack – 'Keeping it Real

"What happened in your game, anyway?" Jamie asked Jack. He'd had enough of talking about his match and why he'd been substituted; it wasn't going to change anything.

"What do you think?" said Jack, throwing him the contagious grin that always made Jamie smile too. "Let's put it this way – you aren't the only one with a Cup Final to look forward to!"

As they walked home and Jack told Jamie how she'd saved a penalty to send the girls' team through, Jamie felt even closer to her than normal. She didn't seem to think any less of him because he'd been substituted. He could probably even score an own-goal in the Cup Final and know that she would still feel the same way about him.

Jamie put his arm around her shoulder. He liked doing that when they were out together. It made him feel proud.

"Can I stay at yours tonight?" he asked. "I can't be bothered to go back to mine. It doesn't even feel like home any more now. Not with *him* there."

"I told you," said Jack, lightly squeezing Jamie's hand. "My mum says you shouldn't stay over any more, now we're . . . older. We'll do something on the weekend, yeah? And anyway, what's wrong with your place? I thought you liked Jeremy."

"I used to. . ."

11
In and Out

Jamie put his key in the top lock and twisted it. He hoped the door wouldn't open, which would mean that no one was in. But it did. That meant that *he* was home. *He* being Jeremy.

Jeremy had moved in about three months ago. At first it had been all right; Jamie had liked seeing his mum happy. But now it was as if Jeremy thought he was in charge of the whole house. Whatever he said went.

The most annoying thing of all was the fact that he kept saying that Jamie wouldn't make it as a pro. He called it a "pipe dream" and said that sooner or later Jamie would have to grow up and think about getting a job in the "real world".

Jamie wished he'd keep his opinions to himself. He

didn't know anything about football and he wasn't even Jamie's dad. Why didn't he just stay out of it?

Jamie's legs were aching. Even though he'd only played half the match, he'd had to do the work of two players in that stupid wing-back role that Hansard had made him play.

He felt like slumping into the sofa and watching football on TV. Foxborough – the best team in the country – were playing tonight. The match started at eight. But, as he walked into the kitchen, Jamie could hear that Jeremy was already in the lounge watching his own programme.

This was supposed to be his home but Jamie couldn't even watch what he wanted on the TV.

Jamie grabbed an apple from the fridge – he had to get to the nice green crunchy ones before Jeremy did – and then he left the house. He didn't bother saying hello. He just wanted to get over to Mike's.

At least he could watch the football there. In peace.

12

"Step, Shave and Knock!"

"It doesn't work like that, JJ!" said Mike as they tucked into their toasted cheese sandwiches – Mike's speciality – in front of the football. "Just because Dillon's been spotted, it doesn't mean that you won't be.

"And, anyway, you're a late developer, aren't you? You're only just starting to get your growth spurt."

Jamie was glad Mike hadn't used the word "puberty". Jamie hated that word. It sounded like a word a doctor would use.

But it was true – he *had* started to grow quite a lot

over the last few months. His school trousers were now starting to get too short for him and he was practically the same height as Jack now, which made things easier.

His hair had started to change colour too, deepening from red to brown.

Jamie licked up a strand of melted cheese which had got stuck to his chin. He wondered how tall he was going to be when he was older. He couldn't remember how tall his dad was – it had been such a long time since he'd seen him, and his mum had thrown away practically all of the pictures of him.

What if his dad was really tall? Would that mean that Jamie would end up being really tall too?

He would love it if he ended up being bigger than Dillon! He imagined meeting Dillon again when they were both older and him going up and pushing Dillon in the chest. "What's the matter, Simmonds?" he'd say, as Dillon stared up at him trying to work out who this giant was. "Don't remember me? Does the name Jamie Johnson ring any bells?"

Then Jamie's tall story was interrupted by the commentator on the TV, who was going mad because the youngest player on the pitch had just scored on his debut for Foxborough. He was only seventeen.

Suddenly Jamie didn't feel hungry any more.

"See, Mike?" he said, as though everything was

somehow Mike's fault. "This guy's only three years older than me and he's already making his debut – and scoring! I'm way behind. I've blown it!"

"What are you talking about, Jamie? You've got a Cup Final to come in less than a week. If you're ever going to turn it on, that's the game to do it in. If there were scouts there today, they'd be mad not to come back for the Final."

Jamie licked the roof of his mouth. It was burnt. Mike did have a point, though. The Final – that could change everything.

"Maybe you're right," Jamie said, going to get a glass of water from the tap. "But even if they are there, what's to say they're going to be impressed by me? I mean, I couldn't even beat a man with my step-over today. How can I be a professional winger if I can't do a proper step-over?"

Jamie looked at Mike, who was pushing his hand back through his greying hair. Jamie wondered what he was thinking.

"Remember when we went on holiday and you met that mouse with the huge ears?" said Mike, pointing to the photo of Jamie and the mouse on the wall.

"Yeah, course I do," said Jamie. "That was my first proper trip away." Stopping to look at the photo, he couldn't believe how big his front two teeth had been when he was younger. But they were OK now.

"That poor guy in the mouse suit. You kept going on about his big ears!" smiled Mike.

"I know I did," said Jamie, barging his granddad's shoulder as he sat back down on the sofa. "But I'm not being funny, Mike – that was ages ago. I'm not a kid any more, you know. I'm serious, I need help with my step-overs, not talk about a mouse with big ears!"

"But who said the two aren't connected, eh, Jamie?" said Mike, a little mysteriously. He still had his eyes focused on the TV. Foxborough were playing some great football.

"What are you chatting about, Mike?"

"I'm saying that maybe that mouse and his ears can help you with your step-overs."

Jamie was mystified.

"Look," said Mike, turning down the volume on the TV. "Bring that pad over here." He was pointing to the square stack of sticky notepaper he kept by the phone.

Jamie went and brought it over. It had lots of doodlings and telephone numbers on it. Mike had even been practising his signature on it!

"Right," said Mike. "Take a fresh piece and draw me a picture of the mouse's head with his nice big ears."

"Fine," said Jamie.

He didn't have to think too hard. All he had to do was look at the photo on the wall. He did a quick sketch and handed it over to Mike.

"Not bad," said Mike, laying the drawing on the table between them. "But maybe you're right. It was ages ago that we met him. Maybe he needs you to bring him up to date a bit. How about you give him a new crew cut? And, in return, he can help you with your step-overs."

"He can what?" Mike's advice was normally spot-on, but Jamie wondered if he'd actually lost it this time. How could giving an imaginary haircut to a drawing of a mouse help Jamie with his step-overs?

"It's simple, JJ. If you step on his ear, shave his head and then knock him away, you'll be able to do your step-over."

"Mike, what are you—"

"Trust me, Jamie. Just say it. You're going to step on his ear, shave his head and knock him away."

"Fine, I'll step on his ear, shave his head and knock him away. Happy now?"

"Again," said Mike.

"I'll step on his ear, shave his head and knock him away. And then I'll be able to do a step-over."

"Good," said Mike, taking the pen from Jamie's hand. "So what we're saying is, you're going to:

"Step on his ear with your left foot.

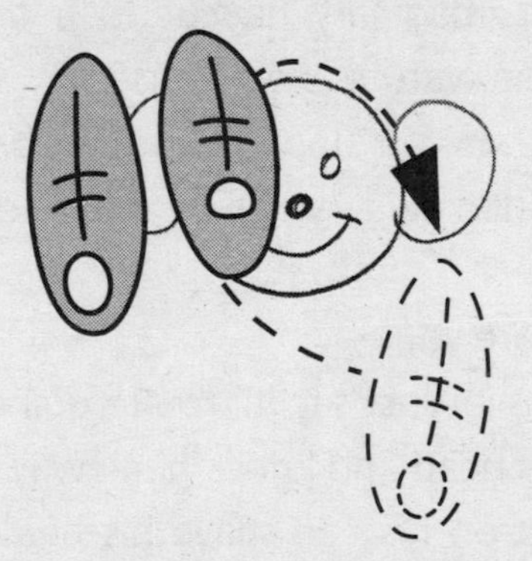

"Then shave his head with your right foot.

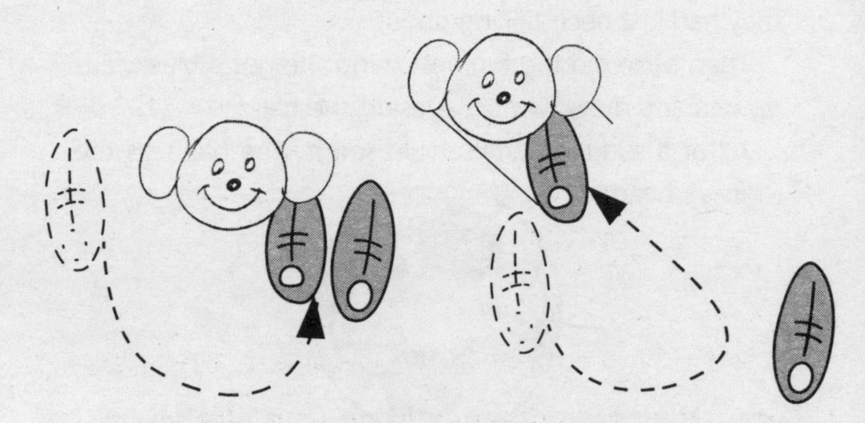

"And then knock him away with your left foot.

"Get it?" said Mike, getting up from his seat.

"Sort of."

"Remember, it's simple: step on his ear—"

"I know, shave his head and knock him away."

"That's it," said Mike, moving cushions and chairs out of the way to make some room. He got a ball from the cupboard under the stairs and put it down on the carpet.

"Are you ready to have a go?"

"But I don't—"

"Yes, you do, Jamie," said Mike, smiling. It was as though he knew something Jamie didn't. "Your feet know exactly what to do."

Jamie stood over the football and stared at it. He still couldn't see the connection between the ball and what they had just been talking about.

Then Mike did the funniest thing; he got a black felt-tip pen and drew two big eyes on the ball.

All of a sudden, Jamie could see it. The ball was the mouse's head!

Without thinking, Jamie put his left foot over the ball, where the ear would be, swished his right foot around the ball as close as he could to shave the head and then brought his left foot back to knock the ball away.

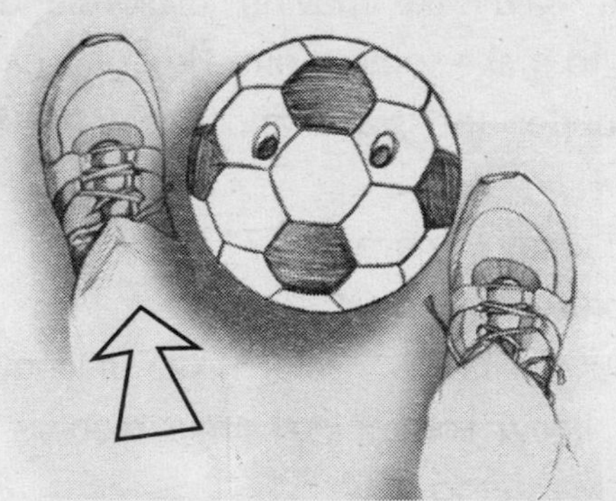

Step on his ear.

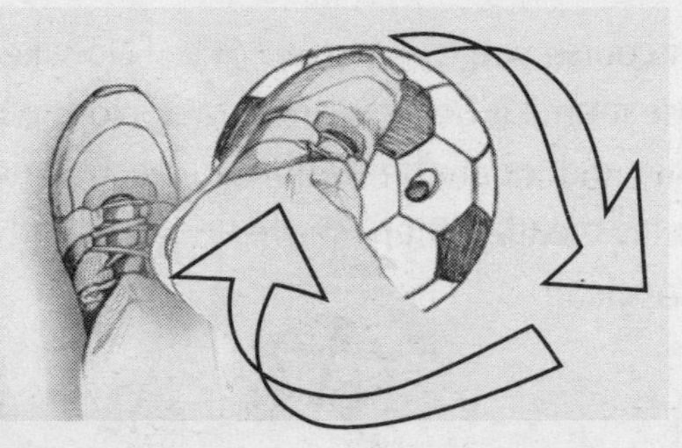

Shave his head.

Knock him away. As he did it, he just knew; it was the perfect step-over.

"That's it!" said Mike. "And explode away when you go!"

"I can do this!" said Jamie, dragging the ball back into position to do another one.

"Of course you can," said Mike. "Now keep doing it; practise it until it becomes natural to your whole body."

Jamie did one after another, each time repeating under his breath: "Step, shave and knock ... step, shave and knock."

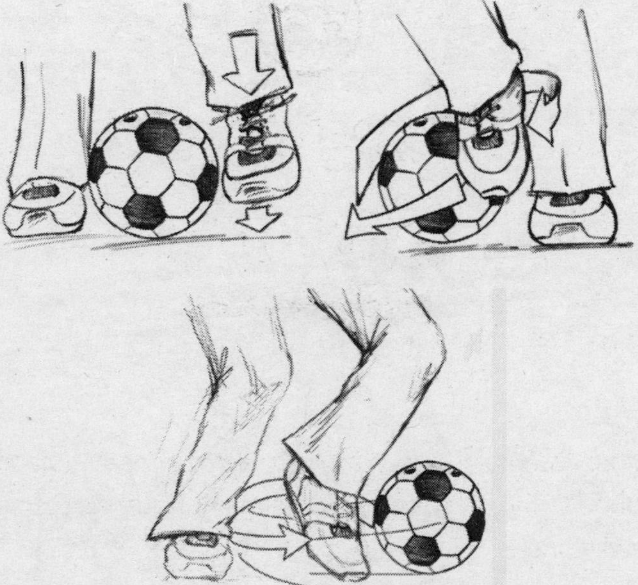

After a while, his feet seemed to work by themselves. They knew how to do a real step-over.

"Looking good," said Mike, going to make himself a cup of tea. "Reckon you'll use it in the Cup Final?"

"Might just do that!" said Jamie, proudly. Then he swapped over to work the trick on his other foot.

13 Scrappy Start

Friday 23 May

Before Assembly, there was a big crowd of people standing around Dillon. It was as if he'd already made his debut for Hawkstone.

Jamie sat down and tried to read the sports pages of his paper. He wanted to work out how many points Hawkstone were behind Foxborough in the league table. It was impossible, though. All Jamie could hear was Dillon's voice.

"Yeah, I'll have an agent soon," he was saying. "They'll sort out the contract and everything – I'll just turn up and play."

"Wow, that's so cool!" said a group of girls who had joined the crowd. They were pushing one another to get closer to Dillon. "How much money are you going to earn?"

"A lot. And the best bit about it is that it's the stupid fans like him who'll be paying my wages!"

Jamie didn't have to look up to know that Dillon was pointing at him. He could feel his forehead burning as he sensed everyone's eyes on him.

"Poor old Johnson," Dillon continued. "Sooner or later he's got to accept the fact that he just ain't gonna be a player. That's it, mate – you read about the professionals. You're never gonna be one."

Jamie ignored him and turned the page of the newspaper. It was best not to get involved; whenever he and Dillon had a fight, it was always Jamie who ended up coming off worse.

"You'll go to watch Hawkstone with your *granddaddy* and you'll be cheering me on when I score a goal. You'll probably even tell people you know me!"

The group around Dillon were starting to laugh. Even the girls. Jamie tried to force a smile to make it look as though he didn't care what Dillon said. He knew one thing, though: he would never cheer anything that Dillon did. Ever.

"I mean the only person that actually likes him is

Jack – and she's way too fit to be going out with a minger like him! I might have her myself, actually. Footballers can get any girl they want. And she needs a real man, not a—"

That was too much.

"Yeah?" said Jamie, putting his paper down and snarling fiercely at Dillon. "And why would any girl be interested in someone with big, fat spots all over their face?"

"Oooooh!" the group around Dillon said in unison. They cleared a space between Jamie and Dillon. "Fight! Fight! Fight!" they started chanting.

"No girl would come anywhere near you," Jamie carried on, getting up from his chair now. "I've seen you pick your nose and eat it! And your breath stinks!"

"That's cos I've been kissing your mum," Dillon laughed. "And she's—"

Without even realizing it, Jamie had launched himself at Dillon. His head was swarming with anger.

"Come on, then. Let's see what you've got," Dillon taunted.

But as Jamie rushed towards Dillon, he felt his legs tangle beneath him and he fell over.

Dillon had tripped him up and now, as Jamie lay prone on the floor, all he could see above him was Dillon's ugly face snorting with laughter.

"When will you learn?" he sneered. "You're a skinny

little runt and you shouldn't mess with people that are stronger than you."

Dillon's words stabbed Jamie's brain. Anger and embarrassment spread through him; everyone had seen what had happened.

Then Dillon turned to the group that had been watching the whole time. He pointed at Jamie and said: "No wonder he'll never be a footballer! He can't even stand up!"

14

Professional Ambition

"Believe it or not, some of you are going to have to think about your careers soon," said Miss Claunt, writing JOBS & QUALIFICATIONS in big letters on the whiteboard.

Jamie was drawing the moves to his step-over on the back of his exercise book. He'd promised himself that he would visualize the skill every day between now and the Cup Final. He wrote the words "step, shave and knock" as neatly as he could above his sketches.

Ollie Walsh, who sat in front of Jamie, must have sensed that he was thinking about football. While Miss Claunt was talking, Ollie turned his back to her and said to Jamie: "We gotta get the paper today – see if our picture's in there!"

"Ollie," Miss Claunt said calmly. "Can you turn around, please?"

Ollie raised his eyebrows to Jamie and just completely ignored her. He seemed to have this spell over her that allowed him to do whatever he wanted.

"Can you imagine what it's gonna be like playing at Phoenix Park!" Ollie continued, as if they were having a chat on a football pitch, not in the middle of the lesson. "It gonna be—"

"Ollie!" said Miss Claunt, now raising her voice. "I asked you to TURN AROUND!"

Then Ollie did something that was either very clever or very naughty. Probably both.

He stood up, looked at Miss Claunt straight in the eye, turned around in an entire circle and sat back down again, still keeping his back to her, facing Jamie.

Jamie was laughing and so was the rest of the class.

"What?" said Ollie, the picture of innocence. "She asked me to turn around! That's what I did."

"OK – very clever, Ollie. Can you turn *this* way, please," said Miss Claunt. Jamie could see that she was almost smiling. He was surprised that she wasn't more angry. Then again, this was Ollie. She never got angry with Ollie.

"Thank you, Ollie," she said, pulling her fringe to the side of her reddening forehead as Ollie finally turned to face her. "So sorry to interrupt your conversation."

"No problem, miss."

"Now, since you're in such a talkative mood today, Ollie, perhaps you'll be kind enough to share with us the career that *you* would like to have when you're older?"

"Sure, miss. I'm going to be a federal agent."

"And do you even know what that means?"

"Yeah, it means you get to wear a badge, be on TV and pull loads of girls. That's my kinda job!"

Everyone started laughing but Miss Claunt carried on, still trying to make her point.

"I'm sure you would make an excellent federal agent, Ollie – you've certainly got the self-confidence – but you know you'd need top marks in all your exams to be accepted into the intelligence services. . ."

Jamie drew a football on his book. Then he started to sketch in the mouse's eyes and ears.

". . .about you, Jamie?"

Jamie looked up blankly. He hadn't been listening.

"I asked you what career you're interested in, Jamie."

Jamie should have just said doctor or dentist but, before he'd allowed himself a second to think about it, he'd already blurted it out: "Footballer, miss. I'm going to be a footballer."

The class started laughing again and Claunt marched over to Jamie.

"Show me your exercise book," she demanded.

"Why, miss? I—"

"Let me see it!"

Jamie handed it over.

"Not that side! The other side! The one you've been scribbling over all lesson. . . And what's this?" she shouted, holding the book up so the whole class could see Jamie's step-over sketches.

"It's a . . . football skill, miss . . . I just had it in my head . . . I was still listen—"

"Right – that's it!" said Claunt. "I'm not having people sitting here drawing cartoons in my lesson. I've had enough. Get out!"

"Ah, sorry, miss," said Jamie. "But it's the truth! I *am* going to be a footballer!"

Again the class started laughing, which only made Claunt angrier. Now there was no way she was going to accept his apology.

"I don't care what you think you're going to be!" she screamed. "You can tell the head teacher when you explain to him why you've been sent out! Now get out!"

15 Familiar Face

Ian Reacher was in an empty cafe. He had just got back into town. He had been away for a long time, but now there was a reason to come back. He put down his coffee and stared hard at his newspaper. He couldn't take his eyes off that boy's face in the team photo at the end of the line; the one that was so familiar to him.

He read the story again:

Friday 23 May

Sport

Kingfield Boys Through to Phoenix Park Showdown

Advertiser Picture Exclusive

Stars of the future set to make their mark in Cup Final

He looked at the boy's fair, reddish hair. His face was older now than the last time he had seen it. The boy was beginning to turn into a man.

But when he stared into the boy's eyes, he recognized the same brooding ambition that had always been there.

Yes, he was sure he was looking at his son's eyes.

They were Jamie Johnson's eyes.

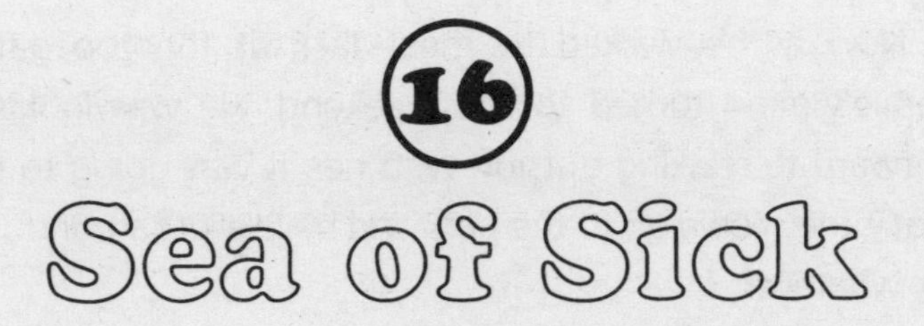

16 Sea of Sick

It was 4.30 by the time Jamie eventually got out of school. Mr Patten, the head teacher, had given Jamie the worst punishment for being sent out; he'd had to clean the floor of the boys' toilets.

It was disgusting: none of the boys lifted up the toilet lid when they did a wee. They seemed to spray all over the floor. It was sticky and smelly with yellow stains everywhere.

What had made it even worse was that Hansard had walked past just as Jamie was scrubbing the floor. "You've missed a bit, Johnson," he said, almost gleefully.

Jamie felt like chucking the stinking cleaning rag right at Hansard's face but, for the sake of his Cup Final place, he didn't.

When Jamie had told Jack about his punishment and that he'd be late out of school, she'd laughed. "Don't worry," she'd said. "I'll wait for you – as long as you promise not to touch me until you've had a shower!"

Now as he walked to meet Jack at the top gate, Jamie's mind turned to the weekend. He was looking forward to relaxing outside with her. It was going to be hot – they could go to the park and have a kickaround . . . or whatever.

But as Jamie got closer to their meeting point, he was met by a sight that made him feel physically sick. Jack was there as she'd said she would be – that wasn't the problem. The problem was she that wasn't alone – Dillon Simmonds was with her.

He was leaning with his hands on the wall above Jack's head. He was standing so close to her that Jamie couldn't see her face.

Jamie's insides were twisting around themselves. Dillon had found Jamie's weakness: Jack.

"Come on, no one's looking," Dillon was saying as he grabbed Jack's left hand.

Jamie's stomach lurched further into a sea of sick.

"I know you want to," Dillon said. He was whispering his poison into her ear. "You can say you got off with a professional footballer."

Jamie didn't have to watch any more of this. He

couldn't. If they wanted each other, they could have each other. Jamie would get his revenge on Dillon one day and when he dumped Jack she'd regret it all right.

He turned around and crossed the road to walk on the other side. He didn't want either of them to see him.

But why was *he* the one that felt embarrassed?

17

Oi, Grumpy!

As he walked home, Jamie thought back over everything that he and Jack had shared since that first day they had played together when she moved into his road.

Maybe he would never have a friend like her again in his whole life.

A small tear pricked the corner of his eye but he wiped it away angrily. If she was prepared to throw it all away for some stupid bully, he'd obviously never really known her in the first place. Maybe Jamie was the *real* idiot.

"Hey! What happened to you?" said Jack, sprinting up behind him. "I waited for you for ages!"

Jamie ignored her and upped his pace. He was trying to think of something to say that would hurt her as much as she'd hurt him.

"Oi, grumpy!" she said. "How were the toilets?" She was laughing now.

Jamie blanked her again. He was nearly home now.

"Jamie!" she said, sounding worried. "What's happened?"

"Have a nice time with Dillon, did you?" Jamie's voice faltered as he said Dillon's name. It went higher, and he sounded like he used to before his voice had broken.

"What?" said Jack, tucking one of her dreadlocks behind her ear.

"You heard me. If you wanted to get off with him, you should have just said. It's fine. . . Just don't expect me to. . ."

"Ah, you're jealous! That's so cute."

"I'm not jealous and I'm not cute. You can't get out of it by—"

"Jamie! Will you shut up for a second! Look, he came up after school and started chatting his usual load of rubbish. That was it. I wanted to push him away but I didn't want my hands to go anywhere near him so I let him say his piece and then go on to the next girl. I'm not interested in him, all right?"

Jamie just shrugged his shoulders. He hoped she was telling the truth.

"Why would I want him when I've got someone a hundred times better?" she said, softly straightening out the collar of Jamie's dirty white shirt.

Jamie was desperate not to smile. He didn't want Jack to know how relieved he was.

"Fine . . . I just thought. . ."

"Well, you thought wrong, Jamie Johnson! Now, are we cool?"

"Yeah, Jack Marshall. . . Yeah, we're cool."

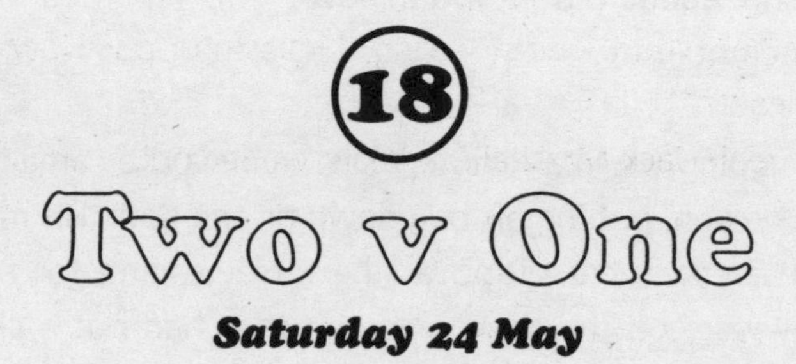

18 Two v One

Saturday 24 May

"Jamie!" his mum screeched up the stairs again.

"I said, in a minute!"

The more she shouted, the harder it was for him to concentrate. He was looking at his step-over drawings. "Step, shave and knock," he said to himself as his feet flashed around an imaginary ball. He'd stuck them to his bedroom wall so they would be the last thing he saw at night and the first thing he saw in the morning. He packed his boots and a towel into his bag and opened his bedroom door.

"This is what happens if you're too soft on him," he could hear Jeremy saying. "It's time for you to try tough love."

"But he's my baby, I can't help it."

Jamie banged his door shut and stomped down the stairs. He wanted them to know he'd heard them talking about him. "Tough love," he repeated with contempt.

"I'm going out in a minute," said Jamie as he came into the kitchen, putting his bag down on the floor. His mum and Jeremy were sitting at the table waiting for him. They were on the same side and they had put a chair opposite them for Jamie to sit in.

"Take a seat," Jeremy said, pointing to the chair.

"I'm all right," said Jamie. He stayed standing up.

"We'd like to know what all this is about." Jamie's mum said, handing him a letter. It was from the school, telling her that Jamie had been sent out of class for the second time this term.

"It's nothing," said Jamie, handing the letter back. "Just Claunt overreacting again. She probably had her period or something – I dunno."

"Jamie!" his mum shouted. "Don't talk like that. Overreacting to what?"

Jamie sighed. Why did he have to go through all this rubbish? He answered as if he were a robot; with as little feeling as possible.

"She asked me what job I was going to do when I was

older and I told her the truth: that I'm going to be a professional footballer. Then she decided to send me out. That's it. End of story. Can I go out now, please?"

Jamie's mum looked at Jeremy as though she was giving him some kind of signal that they had talked about.

"How long is this going to go on for, Jamie,?" Jeremy asked. He was trying to put on his calm voice.

"How long is *what* going to go on for?"

"This stupid business about being a professional footballer. I'm sorry to have to say this, Jamie, but it's for your own good: IT AIN'T GONNA HAPPEN, And the sooner you realize that, the better."

"Who the hell are you anyway?" Jamie shouted, lashing out at the chair with a violent kick. His face had gone purple with rage. "You don't know anything about football! And you don't know anything about me. You're not my dad and you never will be!"

"You've got to get in the real world, Jamie. I'm only saying this because I care."

"Well, I don't care about you!" Jamie raged, picking his bag up and slamming the front door shut behind him.

19

One on One

"He's probably just doing what he thinks is right," said Jack as they walked to Sunningdale Park together.

"Yeah, but why do they have to have a go at me the whole time?" said Jamie, still fuming. "Why can't they just support me? I mean, I've got the biggest game of my life next week. This is the last thing I need."

"They probably think they *are* supporting you – just in their own way," said Jack. "And don't forget, they don't play football with you like I do. Anyone that's seen you play knows that you can make it."

Jamie smiled. How did Jack manage to make him feel so much better with just a few words?

"Thanks," Jamie said, almost shyly. "And, by the way, I've got a new trick up my sleeve to show you. . ."

*

"Marshall v Johnson," said Jack. She put on her goalkeeper's gloves and then smacked them together. "World Series. Loser buys milkshakes."

"Bring it on!" said Jamie, sprinting over to collect the ball.

They were going to play "One v One". Jack would start on her goal-line and Jamie would start on the halfway line with the ball. Once he kicked off, Jamie had ten seconds to get the ball into the net however he could, as long as it didn't go out of play or Jack didn't have two hands on it.

The scoring was simple. If Jamie got a goal in those ten seconds, it was a point to him; if he didn't, it was a point to Jack.

They both loved the game because it had all the pace and excitement of a full match but they could play this game on their own. Just the two of them.

By the time they got to the tenth point (it was 6 – 3 to Jamie), Jamie was already panting as if he'd just done the school cross-country. He'd been sprinting for the whole game; if he jogged, it just gave Jack the advantage.

Jamie inhaled the warm summer air and put the ball down on the halfway line. He needed one more point to win the "World Series". For a couple of seconds he focused his eyes on the goal and imagined himself scoring. Then he knocked the ball forward and hared off after it. One more touch and he was already level with Jack, who had come to the edge of the area to close down the angles.

At that moment, Jamie's body did something completely by itself. Jamie hadn't even told it what to do.

In a lightning flash, his right foot had circled the ball without touching it and his left foot had knocked it away from Jack. It was his step-over. He must have practised it so many times that his feet now knew how to do it automatically.

Jamie hurdled over Jack's outstretched arm. He was past her. She was a goner. Never coming back from that one.

"Woah!" said Jack, sprawled on the ground. She had surprise painted across her face. "I thought I knew all your moves . . . what was that?"

"Oh, that," said Jamie, rolling the ball into the empty net. "That was my new step-over."

20

Model Mate

Jamie and Jack rolled their towels out along the raised slope on the side of the pitch and lay down.

"Ah, that feels better," said Jack, taking off her boots and socks.

Jamie watched as she stretched out her long brown legs into the sun. She'd lost a bit of weight over the last few months, which had made her more confident. Jamie liked that.

"Do you think I could be a foot model?" she asked, letting her leg rest across Jamie's lap. "I mean, look at my feet, they're still so pretty even though I play football the whole time. Go on, feel them," she said, poking them towards Jamie's face. "Go on – you know you want to!"

"Get off!" said Jamie, tickling the soles of her feet.

"Fine, have it your way," said Jack, standing up.

Now she was strutting down the touchline as if she were a model on the catwalk. When she got to the goalpost, she looked back at Jamie over her shoulder and pouted her lips at him.

Jamie suddenly felt a burst of energy re-enter his body.

"Nice moves," he said, starting to juggle the ball while still sitting on the ground. "But how are your reflexes?"

He leant on his hand and did a bicycle kick, volleying the ball towards Jack. She tried to save it but it hit her knee and bounced away.

For a second they let it roll away, keeping their eyes firmly fixed on one another. They both knew what was going to happen next; it was just a question of who was going to make the first move.

It was Jack.

She sprinted away.

"My ball!" she shouted.

Jamie caught up with her, pulling her back by her waist. "It's mine!" he said.

Jack wriggled free and lunged forward to claw the ball into her clasp.

"Got it!" she said triumphantly. "Keeper wins again!"

"Not quite!" said Jamie, pulling her closer to him to grab the ball out of her hands.

But even now he had the ball, he still didn't want to let her go.

21 Past Glory

Sunday 25 May

Jamie didn't know why he felt this compulsive urge to find out more about Mr Hansard; he certainly didn't have it with any of his other teachers.

There was just something about the way that Hansard had treated him, been so harsh on him right from the beginning, that didn't seem to make sense.

Jamie turned on the computer and checked his inbox.

It was completely full of emails from Dillon. It was the same every weekend.

As he scanned the inbox, Jamie couldn't help but laugh. Dillon literally couldn't spell.

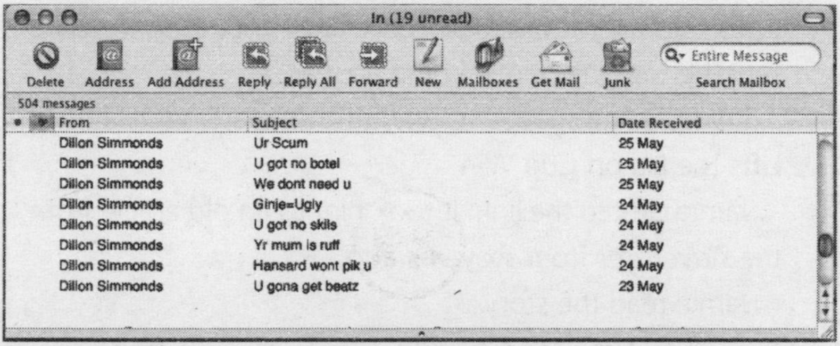

In (19 unread)

Delete | Address | Add Address | Reply | Reply All | Forward | New | Mailboxes | Get Mail | Junk | Entire Message | Search Mailbox

504 messages

From	Subject	Date Received
Dillon Simmonds	Ur Scum	25 May
Dillon Simmonds	U got no botel	25 May
Dillon Simmonds	We dont need u	25 May
Dillon Simmonds	Ginje=Ugly	24 May
Dillon Simmonds	U got no skils	24 May
Dillon Simmonds	Yr mum is ruff	24 May
Dillon Simmonds	Hansard wont pik u	24 May
Dillon Simmonds	U gona get beatz	23 May

Jamie closed down his account. Then he opened a search engine. He typed in the letters HANSARD. For a second, for some odd reason, he wondered if he was doing something wrong. What would Hansard do if he found out that Jamie had been snooping around, trying to find out stuff about him?

Jamie cleared his mind; even Hansard couldn't tell him what to do on his own computer. He pressed the search button.

Hundreds of links came back, practically all to do with politics. Jamie was in the wrong area.

He would have refined the search by entering Hansard's first name but he didn't know what it was. Mr Hansard's first name was as big a secret as the code for the Queen's safe.

Instead, Jamie typed in "Hansard", but this time he linked it with the word "teacher". It was, he realized, the only thing that he actually knew about Mr Hansard – that he was a teacher.

This time far fewer links came back and, as soon as he saw the top one, Jamie knew he was in.

It was a newspaper story with the headline "Hansard Lifts the Lid on Cup Win".

Jamie clicked the link. It took him to an old article from the *Advertiser* from six years ago.

Jamie read the story. . .

Motoring | Travel | SEARCH | Hansard Teache

Hansard Lifts the Lid on Cup Win

Kingfield teacher Mr Hansard has today revealed the tactics that inspired his young football team to win the Interschool Cup for the first time in the school's history.

Speaking exclusively to the *Advertiser*, Hansard – who outfoxed the opposition by deploying a fluid wing-back system – said: "I make the game very simple for my players. I tell them to get the ball out of our area and into the opposition's. Statistically, that makes us the more likely team to score a goal. It's the law of averages."

Hansard, who also teaches maths at the school, was understandably proud that his team scored all five of their penalties on their way to a shoot-out victory, after the Cup Final had finished 0 – 0 in extra-time.

So what was the secret to their perfect penalty shoot-out?

"Precision," smiled Hansard. "Just like mathematics."

"Huh!" said Jamie to himself. He was amazed. Not only had Mr Hansard won the Cup before, but he'd done it playing with wing backs!

Why hadn't he told Jamie and the rest of the team? Maybe Jamie would have shown him a bit more respect. One thing was for sure: if he asked Jamie to play wing back in their Cup Final, there would be no more arguments.

Jamie chucked his sponge ball against the wall. He couldn't wait for the Cup Final. Especially now he knew that Hansard had won it before.

He looked at the picture of Hansard in the article. He'd hardly changed in the six years since it was taken. That was the good thing about going bald, Jamie realized – your hair didn't go grey.

Jamie was just about to close down the article when his eyes settled on the caption underneath the photo of Hansard. He had to read it twice to make sure he wasn't seeing things. The caption read:

The first coach to lead Kingfield to an Interschool Cup win, Hilary Hansard.

Jamie almost fell off his chair. He was laughing so much! Hilary Hansard! No wonder he never told anyone his first name. Hilary was a girl's name!

*

Jamie couldn't wait to call Ollie to tell him about *Hilary* Hansard. He knew he'd love it too.

He was just on his way downstairs to get his phone when the doorbell went.

"Hello," Jamie heard Jeremy say, opening the door.

"Hi," said a voice that sent distant bells ringing in Jamie's subconscious. "Is Jamie in?"

"He's upstairs," said Jeremy. "Can I ask who you are?"

"Of course you can. I'm Ian . . . his dad."

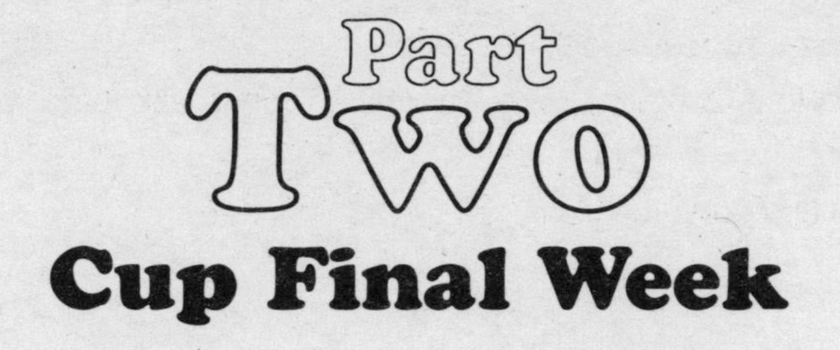
Part
Two
Cup Final Week

22 Right in the Middle

Monday 26 May

Jamie's world had been turned upside down. He was so glad that it was the end of the day and he could walk home with Jack. He really needed someone to talk to.

His mind had been whirring in circles all day. Hearing his dad's voice last night had detonated an explosion in Jamie's head. The fire was still burning.

He'd listened from the stairs to the conversation between Jeremy and his mum when she'd got back from her shift at the hospital.

". . .No matter which way you look at it, Karen, the man has a right to see his son," Jeremy had said.

"He gave up that right the day he walked out on us – with no explanation!" his mum had whispered back angrily. "And what gives him the right to breeze back into Jamie's life just because he feels like it? Jamie doesn't need to know about this now . . . not yet, anyway."

They had no idea that Jamie already knew.

Jamie had lain awake for hours last night. There was so much to think about. He was excited that his dad wanted to see him again, but he felt anxious too.

Where had his dad been? Why had he come back now? And why had he left in the first place?

When Jamie had finally fallen asleep, he'd had a dream – or nightmare – which was so vivid that he could still remember it when he woke up.

In his dream, Jamie was a young boy again. He was five years old. He was walking down the old street that he used to live in and he was holding hands with his mum and dad. He was in the middle of them. He was smiling. He was happy. And so were they.

But as they got to the end of the street, his dad started to turn to the left and his mum started to turn to the right. Neither of them stopped to see which direction the other was going; they both just kept walking and they both kept a hard grip on Jamie's hand as they went.

Jamie was in the middle. His arms were really hurting as both his mum and his dad pulled him in different directions. He was crying out to tell them he was in pain. But neither of them heard him. Or perhaps they just weren't listening.

"Woah! So he's actually back," said Jack, trying to take in everything Jamie had just told her. "Are you OK about it?"

"Yeah, I think so," said Jamie. "I mean, it's what I wanted, isn't it? I guess I'd just never thought about what it would actually be like if he did come back, though. Do you know what I mean?"

"Yeah," said Jack, twisting her finger in her hair as she thought. "Why do you reckon he's come back?"

But Jamie didn't answer the question. He couldn't. All he was able to concentrate on was the man walking down the street towards him.

"Hello, Jamie," said the man as he came closer. He had dark, reddish-brown hair and his face was covered in a huge smile. "Long time no see."

23 Dream-Maker

Jamie couldn't believe it. He hadn't seen his dad for nine years and now, here they were, having dinner together.

His dad had asked him if he wanted to "grab a quick bite and have a chat". At first Jamie hadn't been sure, but then he'd thought to himself: what if he disappears again? I have to take this chance.

Now they were in the cafe together and Jamie was staring at his dad, who was eating his sandwich. Part of Jamie wished he could just come out with it and ask his dad what he'd been doing for the last nine years and why he'd left in the first place, but he didn't want to ruin things – his dad was in a really good mood and Jamie was so excited to see him. He wanted to reach across the table and pinch him just to check that he was really there.

"So, I see your mum's got a new man," his dad said as he took a bite of his sandwich. "How's everything at home?"

"OK, I guess," said Jamie. It seemed so strange and yet so normal to be talking to his dad about stuff like this. "I s'pose the only problem is that I love football and I want to be a professional – but Mum and Jeremy just don't . . . get it."

"Tell me about it," said his dad, squeezing some tomato ketchup on to his plate. "When I was your age, I was in a band with my mates. We were pretty good, could've done something maybe, but all my dad said was: 'Give it up, get a proper job.'"

"That's exactly what's happening to me!" said Jamie. It was so good to talk to someone who actually understood what he was going through. He wondered what else he and his dad had in common.

"By the way," said Jamie. "I'm playing in a massive game on Thursday. It's the Interschool Cup Final . . . you should come and watch!"

Jamie wondered whether he'd said too much. He'd only just met his dad again. Was it too early to ask him to come along to a game?

"Oh, I know," his dad said. "I read all about the Cup

Final in the newspaper . . . I want to know more about your football; what position do you play?"

"Left wing," said Jamie brightly. "I'm the quickest runner in the whole school."

"Really?" Jamie's dad's eyes were sparkling with interest. "A left-winger . . . with natural pace," he repeated.

"Yeah," said Jamie, happy that his dad seemed to care. He was so different to Jeremy. "Scouts came to watch our last game, but the coach—"

"And you're absolutely serious about wanting to be a professional?" his dad said, interrupting Jamie. "You know it's not just about talent; it's about dedication too. You have to really want it."

"All I know is that I want it more than anything else in the world."

"Well then," his dad smiled. "Maybe I can help you."

Jamie practically bounced out of the cafe. He was so happy.

His dad had said that he knew lots of people in football – people who made things happen in the game – and that he'd see what he could do; see if he could help Jamie to get a deal with a club.

Jamie couldn't believe it. It was beyond his wildest dreams.

"Thank you so much," he'd said. "This is the best

thing that's ever happened to me." He couldn't wait to tell everyone – especially Dillon!

"Don't thank me yet – nothing's actually happened," his dad had said. "Look, you concentrate on your football, leave the rest to me. We'll talk after the Cup Final."

Jamie surfed home on a wave of joy. A huge current of hope coursed through his veins.

Not only had his dad finally come back into his life but he was also going to help make Jamie's dream of becoming a professional footballer into a reality.

At last, Jamie thought to himself, everything seemed to be falling into place.

And just in time, too – in three days, he would be playing in the biggest match of his life.

Tuesday 27 May – Last training session before the Cup Final on Thursday

Jamie sprinted out on to the pitch and leapt high into the air.

He had that warm feeling of confidence inside him; he knew he was going to play well.

As he passed the ball with Ollie to warm up, his touch felt secure. Jamie's foot and the ball – they were made to be together.

It had been the same all his life: no matter what was happening, what kind of worries he had, they all seemed to dissolve away the minute he stepped on to a football pitch. When Jamie had the ball at his feet, he was free.

*

"Go on!" Jamie shouted to Ollie, who was on his side in the training match. "Pass it and go for the one-two!"

Ollie looked up and played the ball out to Jamie on the wing before bursting through the middle of the defence to collect the return. Jamie knew he had to get the ball back to Ollie quickly – otherwise he'd be caught offside – but, in the corner of his eye, he was aware of Dillon Simmonds rampaging towards him to make the interception.

Jamie's football brain clicked into gear. There was only one way to get the ball past Dillon in time to play in Ollie for the return; he struck the ball right through Dillon's open legs with enough power to perfectly place it into the path of Ollie's run.

Dillon's head twisted around to follow the ball. He could only watch as Ollie rounded the keeper to score. It had been the perfect one-two with a nutmeg on Dillon thrown in for good measure!

"Beautiful pass, J!" shouted Ollie as they did a high five. Jamie and Ollie would be a difficult duo for the opposition to cope with in the Cup Final.

For the whole training session, Jamie played the role of wing back without a hint of a complaint.

Despite the fact that he felt as if he could go around any

defender today, Jamie didn't do one dribble during the whole session. He just tracked back, marked his man, and struck the ball into the channels when he got possession.

He played it simple – played it Hansard style.

He even resisted the temptation to bring out his most prized new possession – the step-over. He'd save that one for the Final!

It worked, though; after Jamie had cleared a long ball upfield and then run the length of the pitch to try and get up with the attack, Hansard had clapped and shouted: "That's it! Good play. Keep it simple!"

"OK," said Hansard blowing his whistle to bring the practice game to an end. Jamie's team had won 2 – 0. "Gather in," he said.

"Now, the team we're playing on Thursday – Breswell – are a good side; they wouldn't have made it to the Cup Final otherwise. So, if there's one thing that we can be almost sure of, it's that it'll be a tight game. We should be prepared for it to go right down to the wire. Preparation is the key to success and I want us to be prepared for anything."

And, with that, Hansard made every single player line up and take a penalty. He even made the other boys boo and try to put them off as they went up to take their kicks so it seemed like a real penalty shoot-out.

Jamie remembered the article he'd found on the 'net

and how Hansard's old Kingfield team had won the Interschool Cup with a penalty shoot-out. He knew Hansard would be watching everyone's penalty like a hawk, judging them. He knew he had to score.

When it was his turn to take one, Jamie switched off his ears to the shouts and taunts. He only used his eyes.

He stared at the ball and then stared really hard at the bottom left-hand corner of goal. He kept his eyes fixed there just long enough for the keeper to follow his line of vision. Then Jamie stepped forward and swept the ball high into the top right-hand corner of the goal. The keeper dived completely the wrong way. Jamie's plan had worked perfectly.

Even after training had finished, Jamie still had miles of running left in his tank. With two days to go until the Final, his fitness was hitting its peak. His body was perfectly prepared.

Jamie galloped over to collect the furthest ball behind the goal. He flicked it into the air. He wanted to see if he could juggle it all the way back to the halfway line, where Hansard was collecting the kit.

He'd just done a back-heel high into the air and was about to control it on his thigh when Dillon snatched the ball away.

"You think you're good now just cos you do one

flukey nutmeg?" he said, pushing Jamie in the chest. "Well, you ain't. You can't do it in the *real* games. That's the reason you're never gonna be a proper player."

Jamie just smiled and kept on walking.

"That's what you think!" he said over his shoulder. He couldn't wait to see the smug smile crumble from Dillon's face when he heard that Jamie's dad had sorted out a deal for him with a professional club.

"What's that supposed to mean?" said Dillon, chucking the ball at Jamie. He missed.

"Let's just say that you might not be the only one turning pro. . ."

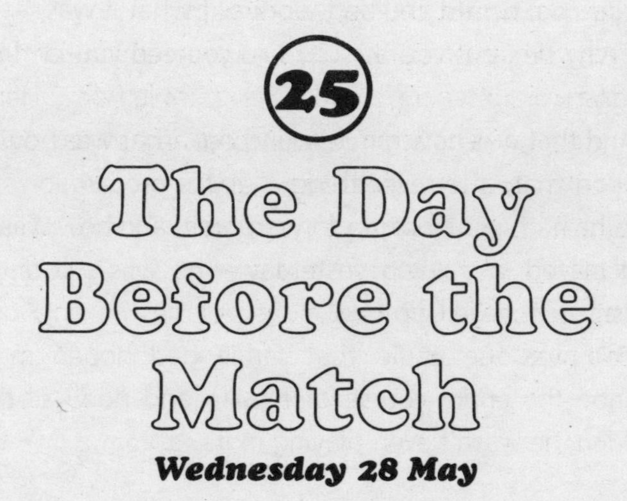

25 The Day Before the Match

Wednesday 28 May

Jamie was just on his way to the notice board to check what time the team coach was leaving tomorrow when he saw Ollie coming the other way.

Ollie was shaking his head. He looked somewhere between mystified and upset.

"Whassup, bruv?" asked Jamie. He was concerned – Ollie was their best midfielder – they needed him in good spirits for the game.

"That's bad, bruv. I don't get it," said Ollie, sucking his teeth. He put his arm around Jamie's shoulder as if he were consoling Jamie for some reason.

"Get what?" said Jamie, his body starting to fidget uncomfortably. He was aware that something bad was happening; he just couldn't work out what it was.

"Why he's put you as sub, J – we need you on from the start. . ."

And that was how Jamie found out. That was how he learned that, after everything – all his preparation, the days he had spent looking forward to it, and how well he had played in training yesterday – he was still only a substitute for the Cup Final.

This was the game that Jamie had hoped might change the entire course of his life and now, all of a sudden, he wasn't even playing in it.

"Yes, what is it, Johnson?" said Hansard, looking impatiently at his watch. He could barely bring himself to talk to Jamie.

When Jamie had heard the news he'd felt like kicking down the door to the staffroom and grabbing Hansard by the throat. He needed to know once and for all what was going on; why Hansard was singling him out . . . . why Hansard seemed to want to hurt him.

Jamie had managed to stay calm enough to catch Mr Gilles on his way into the staffroom and ask him if Mr

Hansard was in there. Now, here they were, standing face to face.

"I just wanted to know why, sir," said Jamie. He searched in Hansard's eyes for an answer.

"Why? Why what?" He was teasing Jamie now, taunting him almost.

"Why you've . . . left me out, sir . . . I don't get it, sir. . ."

"I'm sorry, Johnson – do you think you're so special that you're different to everyone else?"

"No, sir, but it's the Cup Final – I have to—"

"What you *have* to do, Johnson, is accept that I am in charge of this football team and I am not changing a winning side for you or for anyone else."

"Sir!"

But before Jamie could argue, Hansard had gone.

As the staffroom door closed, Jamie sensed that his last chance of becoming a professional footballer might have just been slammed shut in his face.

26

The History

"I just don't understand it," said Jamie. He was practically in tears. "He knows how much I want to play in this final; he knows what it means to me."

"Perhaps," said Mike with a sigh, "that's exactly why he *is* doing it."

Jamie had gone over to see Mike after school. The rest of the day had been terrible. When Dillon had seen the team sheet he'd laughed so loudly that the whole school had wanted to know what was so funny. "Oh yeah, Johnson's gonna be a professional!" he'd shouted sarcastically. "That's must be why he's not even good enough to make it into the school team!"

"But why?" said Jamie, slamming his hand against the

wall. He turned to look at Mike. "What have I ever done to him?"

"Maybe it's not what *you've* done to him," Mike said softly.

"Well, who then?"

"I think that, even after all these years. . ." Mike paused and pursed his lips. "Hilary is still bearing a grudge—"

"Hilary?!" said Jamie. He was stunned. "How do *you* know his name's Hilary?"

"Sit down, Jamie," said Mike. "I think it's about time you knew the truth."

"It was when I was playing for Hawkstone," said Mike, casting his eyes towards the mantelpiece where he kept all his old trophies and photographs. "I was eighteen and captain of the reserves – just on the fringes of the first team.

"One day the coaches brought over this young lad – a striker, sixteen years old – to play in our training session. It was a trial; a chance for him to show what he could do.

"And he was good, very good. He was big, he had presence and, from the first time he touched the ball, you could see he had skill too. All in all, a serious prospect."

Mike rested his head against the sofa and let his mind wander back into the past.

"Anyway, as the centre-half, it was my job to mark him, which I did. I didn't go easy on him, though; I marked him in exactly the same way that I would have marked any striker. When the first tackle came, I wanted to make sure I won it.

"Sure enough, after about ten minutes, this young lad went on a run. He was beating defenders all over the place; it looked like he was going to go all the way. But, just as he approached me, he overran the ball a little. That was my chance. I steamed in for the tackle. We both did. It was a 50/50 and neither of us held back.

"I did hear a crack but I was too focused on winning the ball to take it in. It was only when I turned around after the ball had gone and saw the lad lying on the ground, completely motionless, that I realized what the crack had been.

"The lad had broken his leg in three places," Mike said, grimacing as though he himself were in pain.

"Obviously I was upset. I never went into any tackle trying to hurt a player, so I went up to say sorry as he was being stretchered off. The lad ignored my hand, though, and I'll never forget the look he gave me. His eyes were the angriest eyes I'd ever seen.

"That was it. His trial was over after ten minutes. I heard that he started playing again about a year later, but apparently he was never the same player – he'd lost that yard of pace. That extra bit of speed. We never saw him down at Hawkstone again, anyway.

"He never forgave me for making that challenge, though. He thought that my tackle ruined his chance of making it as a footballer. I suspect he's held it against me ever since.

"You know where this is going, don't you, Jamie?" said Mike, his voice weighed down by regret. "That lad's name was . . ."

Jamie's stomach turned. He said the words before Mike: ". . . Hilary Hansard."

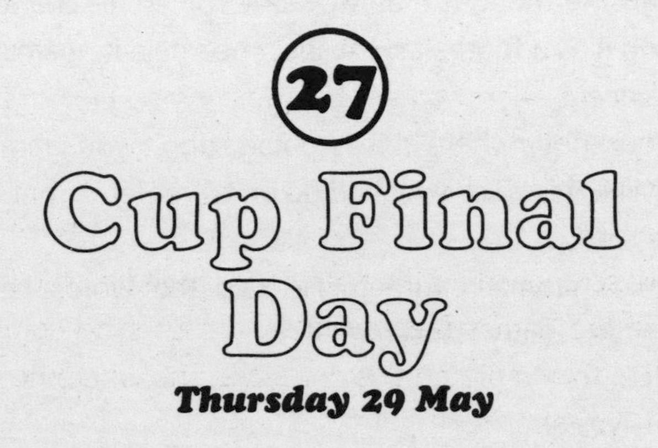

Jamie turned off his alarm and got up.

He had a strange feeling. One he'd never experienced before. It seemed to be an echo of excitement, a shadow of expectation. But not the real thing.

It was the day of the Cup Final. But Jamie wasn't playing.

Slowly and methodically, he put on his clothes. As he did up the buttons on his shirt, he stared at himself in the mirror. He could see now that he was starting to look like his dad.

He was just about to eat his cereal when he saw the

note on the kitchen table:

Good luck today, Jamie!
Guess what? We're both coming to watch you!
We've got something important we want to discuss with you.
All our love,
Mum and Jeremy

Jamie scrunched up the note and volleyed it into the bin. Of all the games they could have chosen to come and watch, they'd picked this one – the one where he was a sub! Typical.

And if the "important" news was that his dad was back, well, Jamie already knew that anyway.

28 Revenge

Jamie looked at the other boys as they waited for Hansard to begin his break-time team-talk.

They were all bristling with energy and excitement. Every one of them was probably imagining scoring the winner in the Cup Final.

Jamie went over to stand by himself in the corner. He looked at his feet. Normally, on the day of a game, he couldn't keep them still. Today, though, they were lifeless. Hansard had killed them.

"OK," Hansard opened. "Here's the team. It's the same one that finished the Semi-Final."

The boys' eyes turned to the whiteboard. There were eleven counters on there, placed in a 5 – 3 – 2 formation. No counter for Jamie.

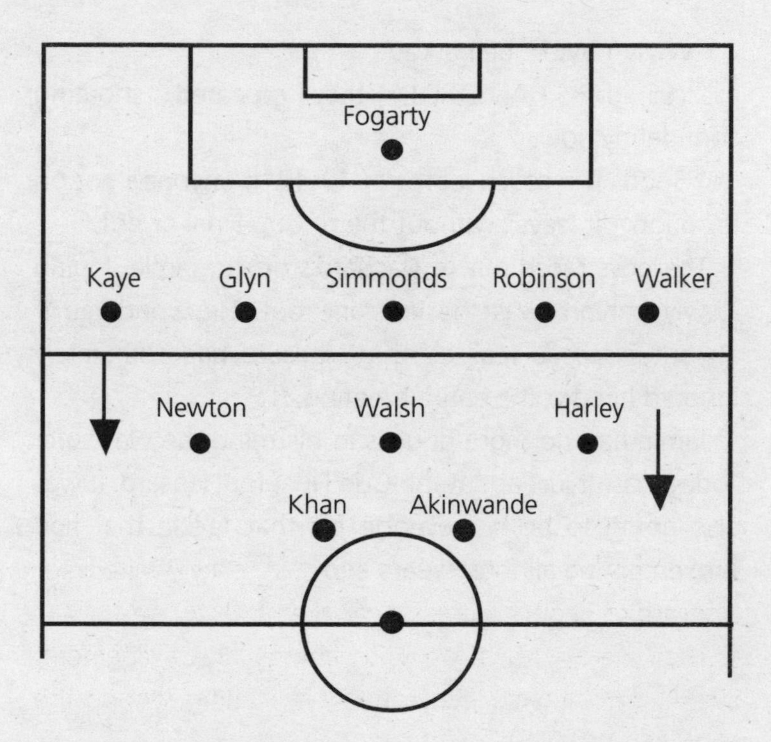

"This team was good enough to win the Semi-Final and it will be good enough to win the Final," Hansard stated, glaring at each one of his players. His words sounded like a threat.

"It will be a battle out there, so we need to play as a unit. Defend together. Attack together. Fight together. That way, we'll win together – won't we?"

"Yes, Mr Hansard," the boys responded, a little hesitantly.

"WON'T WE?" he barked.

"YES, MR HANSARD!" they repeated, shouting confidently now.

"Good. The coach leaves at 12:40. If anyone's not on it, tough – it leaves without them. Cup Final or not."

The boys raced out of Hansard's office. Jamie, loping slowly behind, was the last one out. He wondered if anyone else had realized that Hansard had completely ignored him for the entire meeting.

Jamie had no more doubts in his mind; he was sure. Today wasn't just about the Cup Final for Hansard. It was also going to be his revenge for that tackle that had broken his leg all those years ago.

29
Two Choices

"No way!" said Jack, squeezing Jamie's hand. "If you do that, he wins."

They were having lunch – the school had allowed the boys' and girls' football teams to go in early so they could eat two hours before the matches started – and Jamie had just told her his plan. He was going to miss the team coach. On purpose.

"But there's no point, Jack," Jamie explained. "He's never going to put me on. He wants to take away my chance because he reckons Mike took his. That's what this whole thing is about."

"But if you don't get on the coach, you'll never know. You'll always wonder what would have happened," said Jack.

"It's all right for you," Jamie responded. "You're captain of *your* side. You know you're going to play the whole game."

"Look," said Jack. "When it comes down to it, you've got two options: you can either be a quitter or a fighter."

She got up, put her sports bag over her shoulder and gave Jamie a light kiss on the cheek as she whispered into his ear: "I think I know which one Jamie Johnson is."

30

Bring it On!

Jamie sat next to Ollie on the coach as they headed for Phoenix Park.

Jack was right. There was no way he was giving up. He would never give up.

"This is big-time!" Ollie was saying, fiddling with the netting that was on the back of the seat in front of him. He was practically manic with anticipation. "I mean, if they put us in the paper just for reaching the Final, what are they going to do if we win it?"

It was one of those questions that wasn't looking for a response.

"I reckon they'll have us on TV!" Ollie said, answering himself. "They'll interview all of us!"

"Maybe we'll have an open-top bus ride with the cup

so everyone can come and see us," said Jamie, allowing himself to get into Ollie's frenzied state of mind.

"It's possible, innit?" said Ollie slapping the back of his right hand against the palm of his left hand. "I'm telling you, this is big-time!"

But neither of them realized just how big-time it really was until the coach pulled into Phoenix Park.

All the boys stopped talking as the stadium reared up in front of them. Their mouths gawped as they took in their surroundings.

"Yes! Come on," said Ollie, clenching his fist as tight as he could.

Jamie touched Ollie's fist with his own.

"Bring it on!" they said together. "BRING IT ON!"

And, just for a second, Jamie almost forgot that he wasn't playing.

31
Small Talk

As the Kingfield boys made their way to the dressing room, their opponents, Breswell School, were just arriving.

The first thing that everyone noticed was their height; all the Breswell players were small, and some were even tiny.

Dillon made sure that he barged into practically every one of them as they went past. He wanted them to feel how strong he was.

"Anyone seen Breswell?" he shouted, towering above them. "All I can see is this bunch of midgets! We want a *proper* game!"

Some of the Breswell players were getting wound up but their coach quickly ushered them into their dressing room. "Give your answers on the pitch," he told them as they filed past him.

*

"OK," said Hansard, clapping his hands together as he got ready to send his team out for the big match.

"Today is your opportunity to win a Cup Final," he announced. "You will never get a better opportunity than this . . . But I only want winners out there, so if you don't think you're going to win, don't bother leaving this dressing room."

He let the silence hang for a couple of seconds.

"Good," he said. "Now get out there and win this game!"

"Come on!" the Kingfield boys shouted, banging their fists against the wall as they grabbed their shirts from the kitbag. The school had had new ones made especially for the Final.

Jamie couldn't help but let the excitement in the dressing room envelop him too.

Jamie picked up his shirt and felt its soft material.

"I'll be here all afternoon, lads," said the photographer from the *Advertiser*, snapping away furiously as the Kingfield boys came out of the tunnel and ran towards the pitch.

"If you want to buy any stills, get your dads to call the office."

Jamie's heart shuddered. His dad – Jamie had invited him to come and watch the match! What would he think if he turned up and saw Jamie was only a sub?

He'd think his son was rubbish. He'd forget trying to get Jamie a deal with a professional club. He might even take off again.

Jamie couldn't allow that to happen. It was only now, with his dad back in his life, that he'd realized how much he'd missed him all these years . . . how much he needed him.

Jamie understood that there was no alternative; he *had* to get himself on to that pitch today. Now he just needed to work out how.

32

A Wish on the Pitch

"And welcome to Kingfield School!" boomed the PA announcer as Kingfield took to the Phoenix Park pitch.

"Yeah! Go on Kingfield!" responded the crowd.

Jamie turned around to see there were about three hundred people in the stands to watch the game. It was by far the biggest crowd he'd ever played – or rather been a substitute – in front of.

He looked to see if he could spot his dad or his mum and Jeremy but, with everyone jumping up and down, it was impossible.

Now both sides were on the pitch, warming up. If

Jamie were out there, he and Ollie would be spraying long passes to each other.

The tension was mounting as the referee called both captains to the centre circle to toss the coin.

On the sidelines, Jamie bent down to touch the pitch. It felt perfect. He picked up a couple of blades of grass and rolled them between his thumb and his fingers. Then he stood up and released them.

As he watched the blades flutter to the ground in the hot, windless summer air, Jamie made a wish inside his head. He hadn't done that for a very long time.

"Over here, Jamie!"

Mike had somehow managed to get himself down to the side of the pitch. He was standing next to the corner flag.

As Jamie wandered towards him, the referee put his whistle to his mouth and blew to get the game under way.

Mike must have seen Jamie's face drop because he put his arm around his grandson and said: "Don't worry, JJ. You'll get on and, when you do, you'll be the best player on that pitch."

INTERSCHOOL CUP FINAL
PLAYED AT PHOENIX PARK
KINGFIELD SCHOOL V BRESWELL SCHOOL

Jamie looked on from the sidelines as Ollie slid in and won the first tackle. The midfielder instinctively launched a long ball into the channel for Ashish Khan to chase.

Hansard had drilled the tactic into them over and over again. It had worked against Oak Hall in the Semi-Final but, as soon as Ash and the Breswell defenders got into a race, it was clear the Breswell players were just as quick as him. Ash couldn't get to the ball.

That was a shock. Ash was the second-fastest player in the Kingfield squad. Only Jamie was faster.

The Breswell goalkeeper collected the ball and threw it

out to his full-back Then the defenders began to play the ball between themselves. They had no intention of letting Kingfield get the ball back.

"Let's get into these midgets!" Dillon demanded angrily.

But it wasn't as simple as that. The Kingfield players sprinted forward and put as much pressure on the ball as they could but it didn't make any difference; Breswell just passed faster. They never panicked.

Everything that Breswell did was one-touch. Pass and go. Receive and release. The Kingfield players couldn't get near them. They were being toyed with.

"This lot know exactly what they're going to do with the ball before they receive it," Mike said, nudging Jamie. "That's the sign of a good team."

Soon fifteen minutes had gone and Kingfield had still hardly had a touch of the ball. Even when they did get it, they just punted it aimlessly into the channels for Breswell to reclaim.

"Work harder!" Hansard yelled at his team. He was going red in the face and was getting more frustrated by the second.

Jamie smiled ruefully to himself. The sad thing was, he knew how to make things better for his team. If he could get on that pitch, he could change things; turn the game around.

But, even though he was only standing on the touchline, he may as well have been standing on the North Pole. That's how far away from the action he felt.

Jamie had his face pressed up against the window of the game. Even if he shouted at the top of his voice, no one would hear.

It wasn't until twenty-five minutes into the game that Kingfield managed to win their first corner.

Finally, it was a break from all the defending and chasing that they had been forced to do and it gave Dillon the chance to come up from the back. As he chugged into the Breswell penalty area, it was clear how much taller he was than everyone else. If they could find him with the corner, he'd have a great chance of getting a header in on goal.

Jamie was the regular corner-taker, so when he saw his replacement, Tom Walker, raise both hands into the air as he stepped up to fire in the ball, Jamie knew exactly what that meant – the corner was going to the far post.

Sure enough, Walker whipped it in, hard and fast to the far post. Dillon fought his way through the mass of Breswell defenders towards the ball; none of them were strong enough to stop him. He dived forward, full length, through a flurry of raised boots, stretching every muscle in his body towards the ball, meeting it with a diving header towards the goal.

The crowd in the stands held their collective breath, Jamie stood on his tiptoes to try and see what was happening, then THUMP, the ball smacked against the outside of the post. It bounced away for a goal-kick. Dillon had missed. Just.

The Kingfield players held their heads in their hands. Six inches – that's how far they had been from taking the lead.

"Unlucky!" Hansard shouted from the sidelines, clapping his hands. "That's more like it."

As the players dispersed from the penalty area, only Dillon was left in the box. He was still lying on the ground. At first it looked as though he was just upset he hadn't managed to score. But when the referee started frantically blowing his whistle, it was clear that there was a problem. Something must have happened when Dillon went for the header.

"Can we get a medic on here, please?" shouted the referee. "He's done something to his thumb. I think it might be dislocated."

Dillon was sitting up now, cradling his left hand. Even from where he was standing, Jamie could see that Dillon's thumb was poking out backwards from the rest of his hand. It looked as if it had been stuck on the wrong way.

"He don't need no medics – he ain't a wimp!" said a man, marching on to the pitch. Almost as soon as he saw him, with his big, burly frame and his nose broken like a boxer's, Jamie knew exactly who he was.

The man shoved the referee out of way and grabbed Dillon's hand.

"Let me have a look at that," he ordered.

He took one look at it and said: "Right!"

Then he did something that made Jamie's whole body squirm; the man forced Dillon's thumb right back into its socket. Jamie thought he could even hear the noise of the bone snapping back into place.

"Ahhh! Dad!!!" squealed Dillon, turning his head away.

"Oh, stop moaning, you baby," said his dad, walking back off the pitch. "Wouldn't have happened if you'd have scored."

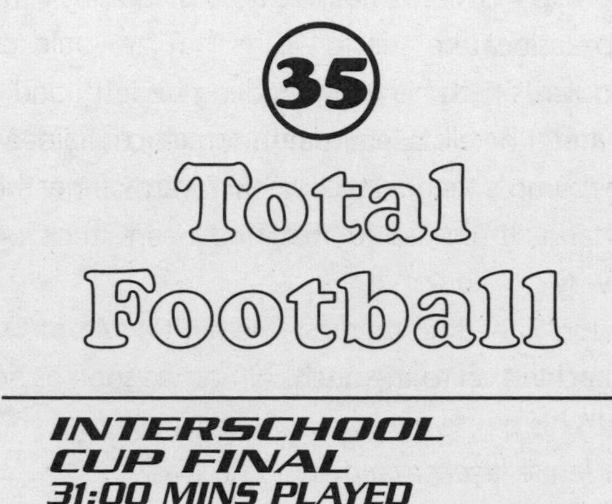

35 Total Football

INTERSCHOOL CUP FINAL
31:00 MINS PLAYED
KINGFIELD 0 BRESWELL 0

Jamie stared at his own thumb, rubbing it softly against his finger. Then he raised his hand to his forehead to shield his eyes from the glare of the sun. He was trying to look for his dad in the stands but he couldn't see him.

Jamie's mum *was* there, though, and she thought he was looking for her. She started jumping up and down and waving back to Jamie. She even blew him a kiss. So embarrassing.

"Look at that!" said Mike, elbowing Jamie in the ribs.

"Breswell's right back has just swapped positions with their central midfielder – that's what you call total football!"

Jamie nodded but he wasn't scared of them. Even though Breswell were by far the best team Kingfield had come up against, he still felt sure that he could cause them problems with his pace.

"Eh, and I'll tell you something else," said Mike, nodding towards the Breswell goal. "Their keeper – have you noticed anything about him?"

"No, why?" said Jamie.

"He never kicks the ball out; always throws it to one of the full-backs. That's because they're trying to keep it on the deck."

The Breswell keeper had the ball in his hands. Jamie studied his movements. He watched the keeper bounce the ball once on the ground and then again, waving the outfield players forward as though he were going to kick it.

But Mike was right – he didn't kick it. Instead, he quickly bowled the ball out to the right full-back, who had dropped deep to collect it. It must have been something that they'd worked on in training.

Jamie wondered how long he would have taken to notice that tactic if Mike hadn't pointed it out.

And, more importantly, he wondered whether Hansard had spotted it at all.

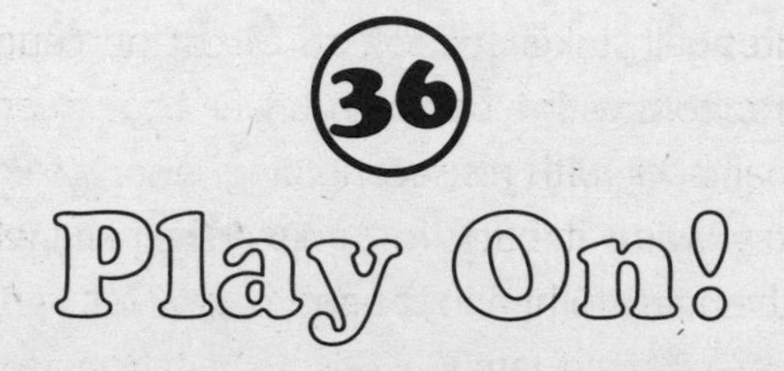

36 Play On!

INTERSCHOOL CUP FINAL
35:00 MINS PLAYED
KINGFIELD 0 BRESWELL 0

After Dillon's chance from the corner, Breswell re-established their grip on the game.

"Get in their faces!" roared Hansard. "They don't like it up 'em!"

Ollie responded by putting in a really hard tackle, going straight through the back of his opponent.

It was too hard a tackle for the referee, though, who blew for a free-kick straight away.

Without taking time to stop the ball, the Breswell centre-half drove a pass into his striker's feet, instantly making a run upfield to support him.

"Rolling ball! Rolling ball!" Hansard protested as Breswell streamed forward. "The ball was rolling!"

"Play on," shouted the referee, stretching his arms out in front of him. "Play on!"

The Breswell striker fended off Dillon long enough to be able to control the ball with his first touch and then lay the ball back with his second.

He was laying it back for the centre-half, who had played the ball into him in the first pace. That centre-half had sprinted the whole way up the pitch, and now he came on to the ball at full pace.

He looked as though he was going to wallop the ball as hard as he could but, right at the last minute, he changed the shape of his body. Instead of smashing his foot *through* the ball, he slipped his boot *under* it instead. He was going for the chip.

Everyone had expected him to go for the pile-driver, including Calum Fogarty, the Kingfield goalkeeper, who had come off his line. Now Calum was caught in no-man's-land, only able to look on helplessly as the shot curved and arced above him towards the goal.

The ball glided gloriously, almost softly, through the air, and, for that second, there was complete silence as all the players on the pitch and all the supporters in the stands watched it follow its seemingly pre-programmed path.

Then the swish and ripple of the net broke the silence as the ball found the top corner.

The Breswell supporters started jumping up and down, celebrating; they were going crazy!

They unfurled a big banner, which read: "Breswell – it's like watching Brazil!"

Meanwhile, Hansard was chasing the referee up the touchline.

"That was a rolling ball, ref!" he shouted. "Bring the play back!"

"I gave the attacking team the advantage," said the referee. "The goal stands."

INTERSCHOOL CUP FINAL
36:00 MINS PLAYED
KINGFIELD 0 **BRESWELL 1**
K McMahon, 36

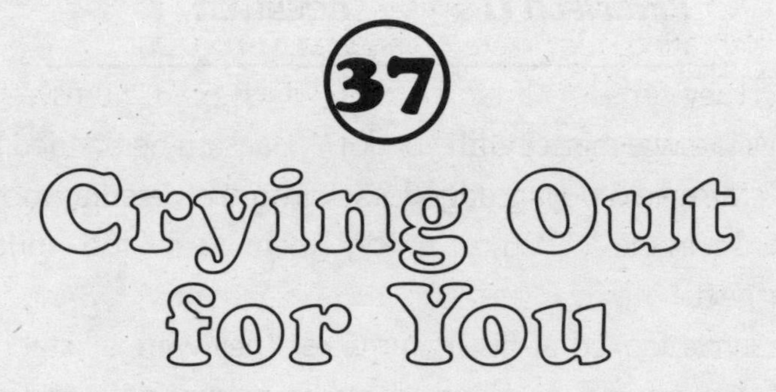

37 Crying Out for You

"Get your top off and start doing your warm-ups, JJ," said Mike, squeezing Jamie's shoulder. It's half-time in a minute, he's got to bring you on. The game's crying out for a player like you."

Jamie smiled.

"Here, hold this," he said, giving Mike his tracksuit top.

He sprinted as fast as he could down the line past Hansard. He was as quick as any of the Breswell players. And as skilful.

He just had to be given the chance to show it.

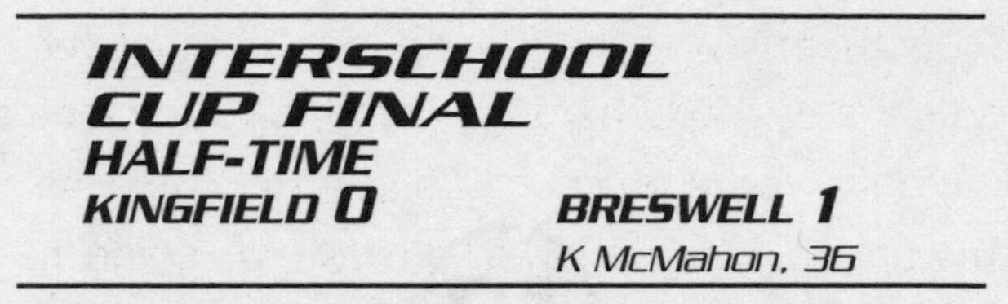

"What's the matter with you lot?" Hansard demanded as the Kingfield boys trudged back into the dressing room at half-time. "You're giving them way too much respect."

Jamie looked at his teammates. They were all staring at the ground as Hansard strode menacingly around them.

Jamie just kept quiet and looked eager. He was sure Hansard was going to make the change.

"We're 1 – 0 down and we're going to do something about this situation," said Hansard.

Jamie stood up and started doing his stretches. He started to feel that tingle of excitement, that buzz that nothing else in the world gave him.

"We're going to try harder," said Hansard. "You're the ones that have got us into this mess and now you're gonna get us out of it."

Jamie sat back down.

"You may think you're good players because you've managed to get to a Cup Final. Well, I'll tell you something: good players – real players – are the ones that show themselves when things aren't going well.

"Football's easy when you're winning. But we're not winning now. We're on course to lose this Cup Final so, what I want to know is, what are you lot going to do about it?"

Time for a Little Shock

"No luck?" asked Mike as Jamie walked back towards him with his head bowed. "He must just be giving them five more minutes. Keep yourself loose, though – he could bring you on at any time."

"Mike," said Jamie. "Give it up, yeah? He's not gonna put me on. He hates my guts. He hates *our* guts."

Mike looked sad.

"I'm sorry, JJ," he said. "I really am. You don't deserve this."

Jamie could see Mike's face redden with anger as he caught sight of Hansard coming out for the second half.

There were two birds circling in the air above Hansard. Jamie prayed that they might splat their droppings all over his bald head.

"I'm going to have a word with him," said Mike, kicking over an empty water bottle. "Maybe old Hilary needs a little shock to help him change his mind."

"No point, Mike," argued Jamie, pulling him back. "If you get involved, it won't change anything. It'll just make it worse."

Mike shook his head.

"He's a small, petty man. What's the point of having a sub if you're not going to use them?"

"Depends who the sub is, doesn't it?" said Jamie. "I s'pose for him, putting me on would be like admitting he was wrong."

"And he's certainly not going to do it with me here," said Mike. "I'm going to the back of the stands where he can't see me.

Mike started to walk away. Then he turned and looked at his grandson.

"And, Jamie, if you do get on that pitch, you show him just how wrong he's been."

Shoot to Win

INTERSCHOOL CUP FINAL
65:00 MINS PLAYED
KINGFIELD 0 **BRESWELL 1**
K McMahon, 36

For a second, Jamie actually wondered if he was invisible to Hansard.

He'd been running up and down the touchline for the last twenty minutes and Hansard had still not so much as acknowledged him. This despite the fact that Kingfield had not even managed a shot on goal yet in the second half.

A line that Jamie had once heard in a movie rose into his brain.

"When you've got nothing, you've got nothing to lose," he said to himself in a rugged voice. Maybe Hansard didn't want to acknowledge Jamie – but who said it was his choice?

Jamie sprinted up the touchline and stopped next to Hansard, putting his foot on the ball.

"Hey – Hilary. . ." he said, sharply and with confidence. He knew this was his last throw of the dice.

"*WHAT* did you call me?!" Hansard's face was divided into the perfect mixture of anger and surprise.

"You used to be a striker, yeah?"

"Yes I did, and don't you dare call me Hil—"

"So why are you such a *defensive* coach, then? Stick me on . . . even you know we've got to shoot to win."

"I'll be the judge of that, Johns. . ."

But Jamie had already sprinted away down the line. He trapped the ball on his calf and flicked it over his head. He could almost feel Hansard's eyes burning a hole in the back of his neck.

40

4-4-2

Just over seventy minutes had gone when Hilary Hansard finally gestured for Jamie Johnson to take off his tracksuit top.

"So you think you're special, then, do you, Johnson?" he said as Jamie stretched his hamstrings.

"I just try my best, sir."

"Right, well, let's see how good your best is, then. Get on there."

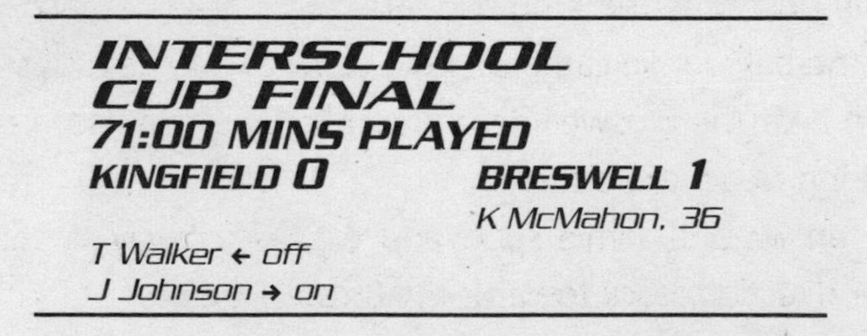

Jamie sprinted on to the pitch as fast as he could.

Being brought on was like being released from a prison of frustration. He'd been impotent on the sidelines. Helpless.

But now he was a part of this Cup Final. He could change things.

As Jamie took his position on the left wing, he saw Hansard come to the touchline, holding up four fingers.

"Kingfield!" he shouted. "Go to 4 – 4 – 2! Attack!"

Jamie smiled. This was exactly what he'd been waiting for.

For the first few minutes, the change in formation seemed to make little difference. The Kingfield defenders were still trying to hoof the ball long. They weren't making use of the width they had now. They weren't making use of Jamie.

Time was running out. They had to start keeping the ball and creating some chances.

"Oi!" shouted Jamie. "Let's get it wide, yeah? I'm free here!"

The next time the Kingfield left back, Steve Robinson, had the ball, Jamie came deep to collect it. As he ran, he could hear the Breswell defender following him. He was marking Jamie too closely.

In an instant, Jamie spun and exploded away in the other direction, back towards the Breswell goal.

"Yes!" he screamed as soon as he made his run in behind.

Steve Robinson had played with Jamie long enough to know what he wanted. He curled the ball down the line, bending it around the Breswell right back. It fell perfectly into Jamie's path.

Jamie collected the ball. He was away. He purred down the line like a brand new Ferrari. He overtook all the defenders in his path.

He put on the brakes just before he reached the byline and dinked over a perfect cross to the far post, where Ash was waiting to receive it. Ash bent back his right foot and unleashed a low, hard volley across the goalkeeper. It was past him. Jamie raised his hands to start celebrating.

And then he put them on his head. The ball had hit the inside of the post and rebounded straight back into the keeper's grateful hands.

Ash kicked the post in frustration. What did the frame of the goal have against Kingfield? What with Dillon's header in the first half too, this was the second time the woodwork had stopped them from scoring.

Jamie wiped a bead of sweat from his forehead. He had an awful feeling that maybe this wasn't Kingfield's day.

Jamie still felt dangerous; still felt as though he could change this game. But he was also aware of the clock's race to the final whistle.

There were now just four minutes left. Jamie wished Hansard had given him more time. What could he do in twenty minutes?

Jamie was stood on the left wing wishing the Breswell goalkeeper would hurry up and kick the ball. He had the ball in his hands and was waving his teammates upfield.

Jamie watched as he bounced the ball once, then twice.

Jamie's mind drifted back to the conversation he and Mike had had about the Breswell keeper earlier. Mike's words rang in his head: "He never kicks the ball out; always throws it. . ."

It was at exactly that moment that, without warning, Jamie suddenly sprinted forward at top speed towards the Breswell goal. The keeper saw Jamie coming and tried to stop himself throwing the ball out, but it was too late; he'd already released it to the edge of the area.

"Man on! Man on!" the Breswell keeper shouted, desperately trying to warn his defender. The Breswell full-back looked around but all he saw was Jamie whizzing past him.

Jamie seared away from him, stealing possession of the ball. The keeper froze in his spot, as if he were a scared animal in front of a car. Then he quickly back-pedalled towards his line.

Jamie sensed his weakness, driving forward into the box.

He was aware of the shouts and screams from the crowd as he dribbled the ball towards the keeper but, deep down, from the very pit of his stomach, Jamie sensed a calmness spreading throughout his body. He felt the cool confidence of an expert doing what he did best.

As the goalkeeper tried to narrow the angle, Jamie

was more peaceful than he had been all day. He was exactly where he wanted to be – in the middle of the action.

Jamie looked at the ball. For a moment, all he could see was a big mouse's face winking back at him. Then Jamie allowed his instincts take over. He let his feet do what had become natural to them and, as they spun around the ball in a mesmerizing whir of skill, he saw his step-over do its job.

The speed of Jamie's spellbinding movements had paralysed the Breswell keeper. He was no more than a statue as Jamie knocked the ball past him.

Now Jamie only had one more thing to do.

He smashed the ball into the back of the net!

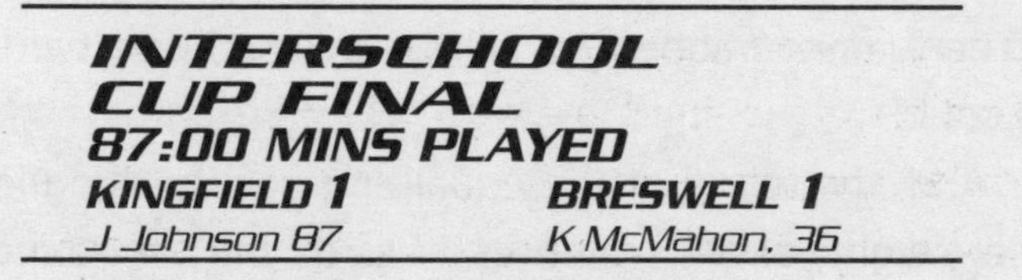

As soon as he saw the ball go in, a thousand volts of electricity tore through Jamie's brain.

It sizzled. It soared with excitement. And release. All of his frustration at having been left out of the starting line-up burned away in his flames of ecstasy.

"Yes!" he shouted as he jumped into the air, punching

his fist towards the sky. "Get in!!!"

His face was bright red. His blood was crackling hot with bliss.

Jamie could see Ollie and Ash closing in on him, wanting to celebrate the goal, but he turned and sped away from them. They couldn't catch him. No one could catch Jamie when he ran his fastest.

Jamie sprinted down the touchline. He was a tornado of released emotion.

When he got to the Kingfield dug-out, Jamie stared straight at Hansard with shimmering eyes of intensity.

He wanted Hilary Hansard to have a good look at the player who had just saved Kingfield from defeat. He wanted to him to know how wrong he'd been to keep him on the bench.

Then Jamie grabbed his shirt and kissed it as hard as he could.

"And, the scorer of the equalizing goal for Kingfield, after eighty-seven minutes," said the announcer. "Number 13, Jamieee Johnson."

"You're damn right it is," said Jamie.

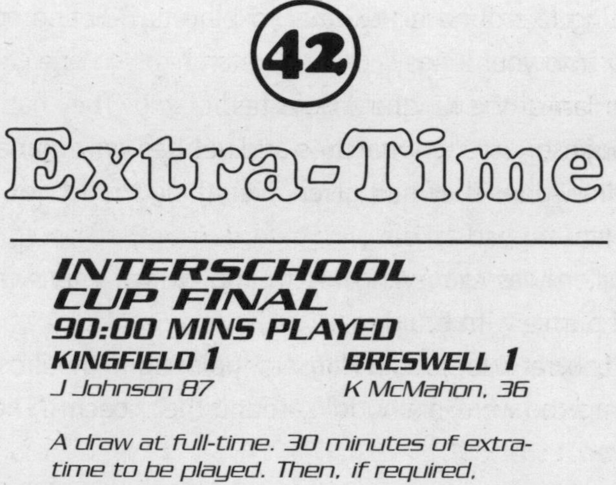

42 Extra-Time

INTERSCHOOL CUP FINAL
90:00 MINS PLAYED

KINGFIELD 1	**BRESWELL 1**
J Johnson 87	*K McMahon, 36*

A draw at full-time. 30 minutes of extra-time to be played. Then, if required, penalties.

As the players from both sides collapsed on to the ground, Jamie looked around.

He still felt strong. He'd only been on the pitch for twenty minutes. He had more energy left than any other player.

He didn't even need a break before the start of extra-time; he wanted to get going right now.

Jamie squeezed his lips together and ground his teeth. A snarling, warrior-like determination was racing through his veins.

The football pitch was his territory. Now he was playing, no one could get in his way.

"Get your breath back," said Hansard, who was walking in a circle around his exhausted players. "Get some air back into your lungs."

A few of the Kingfield boys had cramp. They had run enough to win two matches and yet had only managed to draw one. They had given everything they'd got, just as Hansard had asked.

Dillon was examining his thumb, which was swollen and purple with bruising.

"Look at them," said Hansard, pointing to the Breswell team, who were in a huddle around their coach. "They're scared!"

Jamie poured some water into his dry mouth. He could feel the icy liquid snaking its way down his throat and into his belly.

If the Breswell players *were* scared, it was probably him they were scared of. It had been obvious that Jamie was way quicker than any of them. After he'd scored, one of them had shouted, "Where's he come from?!" and he'd heard them decide to put two men on him.

They could put as many men as they wanted on him. It didn't mean they would be able to stop him.

". . .so now we can go back to 5 – 3 – 2," Jamie heard

Hansard say. "Hit them on the counter-attack."

Jamie spat the water out of his mouth. What? Hansard was reversing to 5 – 3 – 2? But 4 – 4 – 2 was what had just got them back into the game! Why was he changing it now?

"Keep it tight and give nothing away," concluded Hansard. "And if it goes to penalties, so be it. We'll win."

Jamie had his hands on his hips as he waited for the ref to start extra time. He'd had twenty minutes playing as a winger. And in that time he'd scored a goal and hauled Kingfield back into the game.

So what did Hansard do? Go back to 5 – 3 – 2 and make Jamie play as wing back.

He'd obviously never heard of the phrase "attack is the best form of defence".

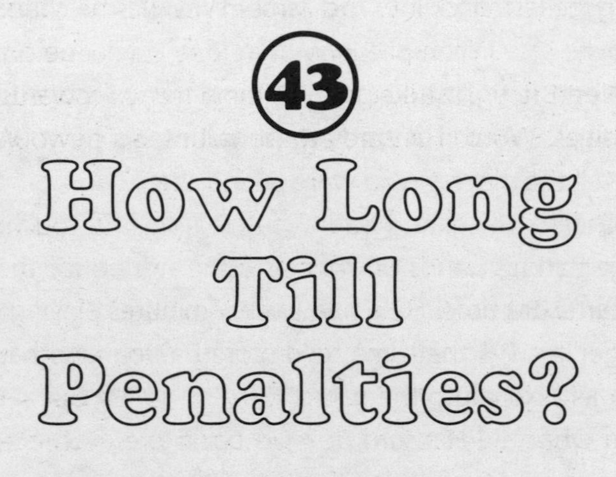

INTERSCHOOL
CUP FINAL
117:00 MINS PLAYED

KINGFIELD 1	**BRESWELL 1**
J Johnson, 87	*K McMahon, 36*

Hansard's plan *was* working in one way: with Kingfield playing more defensively, Breswell were finding it difficult to create chances.

In fact, with only a couple of minutes of the game left and neither side having come anywhere close to scoring in extra time, Jamie realized that perhaps this was precisely

Hansard's plan . . . Hansard *wanted* it to go to penalties. That would be perfect for him – winning the Interschool Cup for Kingfield in exactly the same way that he had done the last time. It would prove his tactics still worked.

As he saw Dillon pile in with a hefty challenge on the smallest Breswell striker, Jamie's mind turned towards the penalties. Would Hansard ask for volunteers or would he just tell the players who were taking them?

"That's it!" Dillon's dad shouted from the touchline, clapping his son's challenge, which had resulted in a corner to Breswell. "Break his legs next time!"

The little Breswell striker sprang up from the ground. He was visibly angry, not just with the tackle but also at what Dillon's dad had said. He started to march over to have an argument with Dillon's dad, who was clearly enjoying the fact that he'd upset an important player from the opposition.

"Hey, Max!" the Breswell coach shouted to his fuming striker. "Forget it! You know how to give your answers."

The striker nodded gravely and turned to make his way into the box for the corner.

Jamie took up his position on the far post. He wondered which end they would take the penalties at.

"Everybody mark up!" Dillon shouted. He took the little Breswell striker that he'd just tackled.

Although Breswell had more skill, Kingfield had won

practically every header the whole game. Now they just had to win one more and everything would go down to penalties.

It was probably because Kingfield had such a height advantage that the Breswell corner taker decided to fire in the corner low. He only hit it at about waist height.

As it fizzed towards the near post, there didn't seem to be any danger . . . until the Breswell striker that Dillon was marking made an electric burst to get to the front post.

Once he'd got there, he leapt into the air, spinning his body around in mid-flight. He looked as if he was doing a karate move, twisting his body to unleash a powerful kick. His strike diverted the ball backwards, towards the Kingfield goal.

Most of the Kingfield players were still taking in the technique that had been required for the little striker to karate kick the ball in mid-air when they suddenly realized that his shot was actually right on target.

"No!" pleaded Dillon.

"Clear it!" roared Hansard.

But it was too late. It was already in.

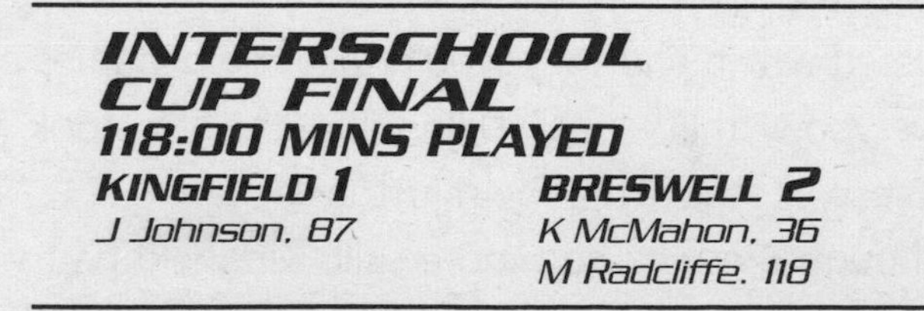

The Breswell players were in a bundled mass of celebration by the corner flag. One after another of their players piled on top.

"Max!" they were shouting. "You've scored the winner!"

Dillon slammed the ball back into Kingfield's net.

"Whose man was he?" he shouted. Everyone knew he was Dillon's man.

"Take the centre quickly!" Hansard yelled, pointing to his stopwatch. "Back to 4 – 4 – 2! Attack! *Attack!*"

Hearing Hansard say they should start attacking now – with one minute left – made Jamie's mouth let out a sound.

He wasn't sure whether it was a laugh or a cry.

Supposed to be a Hero

There was barely time for Kingfield to kick off and punt the ball up towards Ashish Khan before the ref blew his final whistle.

It was over. The dream had ended.

INTERSCHOOL CUP FINAL
FINAL SCORE

KINGFIELD 1	***BRESWELL 2***
J Johnson, 87	*K McMahon, 36*
	M Radcliffe, 118

Breswell beat Kingfield to win the Interschool Cup

All around the pitch, the Kingfield players dropped to the ground.

Ollie had his arms around his legs and was rocking slowly backwards and forwards as if he were in a trance.

Ash was lying flat on his back with his hand covering his eyes.

Jamie sat on the grass and put his head in his hands. This wasn't what was supposed to happen. This wasn't the story he'd written in his head. He was supposed to come on and change the game and lead Kingfield to win the Cup. Maybe even score the winning penalty in the shoot-out. He was supposed to be the hero. Not a loser.

"That was your fault!" Dillon's dad shouted at his son, storming on to the pitch. "He was your man!"

He cuffed the back of Dillon's head.

"Go and get changed, you idiot!"

Jamie shook his head. He wondered if sometimes it was better to have no dad at all than a dad like that.

"You did well, Jamie," said Mike. "I'm very proud of you."

Jamie smiled. He knew that, whatever happened, Mike would always be on his side.

"But we lost," said Jamie, looking on in envy as the Breswell players made their way up the podium to lift the

Cup. "Isn't that the only thing that counts?"

"Eh, you won just by getting on that pitch today," Mike smiled.

Jamie looked over to see Hilary Hansard sloping away towards the dressing rooms. He seemed older now, smaller somehow than he had before the game.

"So where does this leave you and Hansard?" asked Jamie.

"Oh, that's over," said Mike, putting his arm around his grandson. "It was over the minute you came on and scored your goal."

45
The End?

"Hard luck!" said Jamie's mum, ruffling his hair, as she had always done since he was a little kid. "We thought you did some great kicks."

"Thanks," said Jamie, moving his head away from her hand. He wished she wouldn't try to talk about football.

"So, did you get our note that Jeremy and I wanted to talk to you about something important?" she asked brightly.

Jamie wasn't in the mood for talking. He'd just lost a Cup Final.

"Mum – I already know!" he said bluntly. He'd known about his dad coming back before *she* had.

"You know? But how?" she said, a little confused. "We only decided last night."

"Decided what?"

"We're getting married, Jamie! That's what we wanted to tell you!"

As his mum and Jeremy walked hand in hand back to the car where they said they would wait for him, Jamie's eyes scanned the pitch. It *was* big news that they were getting married, but he couldn't think about it now. Not with the remnants of the Cup Final still freshly scattered in front of him.

The Breswell players were draped in one of the big banners their supporters had brought. They were jumping up and down with the Cup, singing: "Championés! Championés! Oh way oh way oh way!"

In front of them, the photographer was snapping away.

"That's it, lads," he was saying. "Cheeky smiles. There's going to be a big splash for you boys tomorrow!"

Jamie couldn't help but think it should be the Kingfield boys up there on the podium. He could almost see him and Ollie lifting up the Cup and then running around the pitch with it. Kingfield had come all this way. And now they were going away with nothing.

Instead of celebrating, Jamie's teammates were silent; some of them were even crying.

It occurred to Jamie that maybe this was the way his professional dream was supposed to end. He'd had his bit of personal glory coming off the bench to score but, ultimately, his team hadn't been good enough to win the Cup Final.

Maybe this was the footballing gods giving him a little nudge. He was fourteen. If it hadn't happened for him by now – and it hadn't happened for him today – it was never going to happen.

Jamie should enjoy his football as a hobby but give up the idea of trying to go professional.

Perhaps that was the real reason that he'd got so annoyed with Jeremy lately. Perhaps somewhere, deep down, he had understood that Jeremy was right. Jamie hadn't been angry with Jeremy. He'd been angry with the truth. . .

The truth that Jamie should start thinking about life in the "real" world.

The truth that the time had come for Jamie Johnson to accept that he would never be a profess. . .

"Well played, Jamie."

He felt a hand rest on his shoulder.

"Dad!" Jamie said. The word slipped out before he could stop it. "I didn't think you were here . . . sorry I lost . . . I—"

"Don't sweat it, Jamie – you were brilliant. We both thought so." His dad gestured to the man standing next to him. "This is my friend Steve Brooker."

"Hello, Jamie," said the man shaking Jamie's hand. He had the firmest handshake Jamie had ever felt.

For a second the three of them stood there in silence until Jamie's dad added: "Steve's Academy Director at Foxborough, by the way."

He said the words so casually, as if he were mentioning that it was forecast to rain tonight.

"What?!" said Jamie. "Foxborough as in Foxborough the biggest club in the country?!"

"Yes," said Steve, laughing. "Well, we like to think so, anyway."

"Oh my God!" said Jamie. His eyes were practically popping out. He couldn't stop staring at Steve. Now he noticed the little Foxborough club badge on his coat. "I can't believe you're actually here!"

"Well, when your dad told me that there was a gifted left-winger playing today, I had to come down and take a look," said Steve. "We're all looking for left-wingers at the moment."

"I'm a left-winger!" Jamie exclaimed.

"I know," smiled Steve. "You're the one I came to see."

46 Something Special

Jamie felt the golden sunlight warm his skin as he listened to Steve Brooker talk.

He wanted to take in every word, hear every syllable that came out of his mouth. Steve Brooker was the most important man that Jamie had ever met.

"I have to admit," Steve was saying. "I *was* a bit surprised that you started on the bench, but then I suppose it was the way that you were able to turn the game on its head in such a short space of time that really caught my eye.

"As a coach, sometimes you only need to see one piece of magic, one passage of play to convince you that there is something you can work with in a player. When you did that step-over today, Jamie, I knew I'd seen something special. Something very special."

Jamie swallowed hard. His mouth was dry. He could feel his head starting to judder with excitement.

"Thanks," he just about managed to splutter.

"Jamie," Steve continued, "I think you might have something. I don't know what it is exactly, but I'd like to find out. I'd like you to come and play for Foxborough."

Very discreetly Jamie dug his nail as far as he could into his own skin. He had to check that it hurt. He had to check that this was actually real. He'd only believe it was if he saw blood coming out of his. . .

"Well?" said Jamie's dad. "Are you going to give the man an answer?"

"Yes," said Jamie, softly at first, still trying to take in everything that was happening. "Yes! A thousand million yeses! I'd crawl all the way up the motorway to play for Foxborough!"

Jamie was bouncing around now, hugging his dad and Steve.

"Great," said Steve. "I'm glad. You'll move up and we'll put you on a Scholars contract. Then, assuming you've done the business, you'll turn pro when you're sixteen."

The words seemed to fly like spirits in the air. They were too precious for Jamie to touch. But he could hear them and he could understand what they meant.

At first his legs went weak and he thought he might faint but then his energy came rushing back. He felt like dancing. He felt like running down the street and kissing everyone he met! He could never have believed when he woke up this morning that his day would end like this.

"Congratulations, Jamie," said his dad. He looked almost as excited as Jamie did.

They hugged for the first time in nine years.

From over his dad's shoulder, Jamie could see a bundle of dreadlocks running towards him.

It was Jack! She must have taken the bus here after her game.

Jamie's face lit up when he saw her. Without Jack, he might never have got on the team coach today. And that would have meant he wouldn't be standing here now, with his dad and Steve Brooker.

Jamie could see Jack was holding something up for him to see. It was a medal! She must have won her Cup Final!

Jamie couldn't say the same. He hadn't won this Cup Final. He didn't have a winner's medal today. But he had something else; something completely different.

He had the future ahead of him that he'd longed for his entire life.

Jamie Johnson was going to be a professional football player.

Want more top footballing action? Catch up on the start of Jamie Johnson's journey to the top.

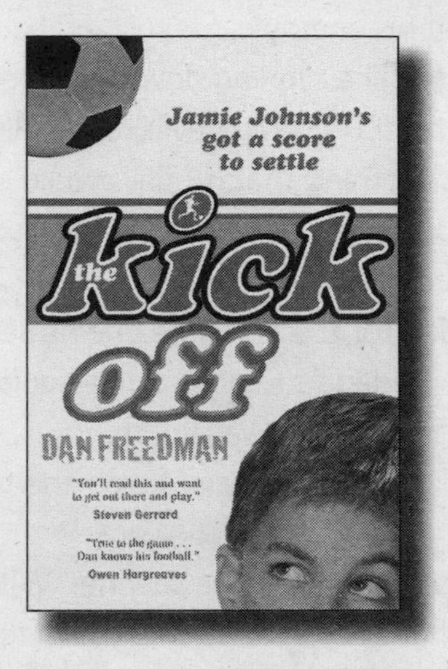

Jamie Johnson's desperate to become his school's star football player (and in his dreams, a top professional too). He's got so much to prove, and not just on the pitch – so why aren't his mum, teachers and best mate on his side?

And don't forget to look out for Jamie's next adventure, coming soon!

To find out more about Dan, football and Jamie Johnson, visit www.jamiejohnson.info